Who Said Women Were the Weaker Sex

by

August Sommers

Twenty-Six Cats

Over the course of the past five or six years I was forced into the unenviable position of being forced out of retirement and made to go back to work.

My previous residence had given me the opportunity at the ripe old age of forty to retire from my traditional servitude. In short a nine-to-five had never been me. My degree meant little aside from sitting in a cubicle rather than standing for eight hours a day. It also meant a few more ducats in my pocket at the end of each month although it wasn't enough to make me have any more of an affinity for my servitude.

And so I found myself in Pittsburgh, Pennsylvania. Now I have never been one to question God's intellect or judgment on anything but should I one of my questions would be why He, in all His magnificence would create Pittsburgh when hell already existed. It just seemed redundant to me.

In any case, and for reasons I do not care to address at this juncture I found myself entrenched in the wet, cold slush and ice that make up a Pittsburgh's winters.

After a year of pounding the pavement every morning in search of employment I was informed that I'd hit paydirt when Children's Youth and Family Services called me to say that I had been selected to become a caseworker for the county. My new family was ecstatic but I knew it was only more of the same. I knew I would soon grow tired of sitting behind a desk in a tiny, little cubicle in a long row of tiny, little cubicles cutting a corner here and there and falsifying documents in my efforts to get the mounting number of cases off my desk while dozens more came flooding in.

It was not long before I began dreading the monotony that was so common in almost every entry level position but like a good soldier I hung in there.

I didn't enjoy many of the drama-filled situations my job entailed but as a people person I did enjoy many of my clients despite the multitude of problems that brought me to know them. I must admit I met quite an interesting mixture of people but let me not digress and get to the crux of my project which motivated me to write this short expose.

You see it was on my last home visit that led to a small epiphany in my thinking. In order to share this with you I would like to theorize on a concept that I have been jostling about for some time now. It is my belief that there is no set standard for so-called 'normalcy' amongst people. Instead we have a loosely bound set of mores, and laws that attempt to regulate and govern people's behavior and with religion as a guideline it is a pretty full-proof plan. Yet, and though it's attempt at setting some sort of guidelines are in effect to limit chaos under a lawless, God-less people it is a superfluous attempt. I therefore conclude that there is no 'normalcy' and that what we have instead is a sort of corralled madness.

For us to even believe that 'normalcy' exists is to underestimate us as knowledgeable and thinking individuals affected daily by various stimuli that in essence shape our experiences and govern our lives. Each of us react differently to these experiences and thus these experiences shape our lives with no real attention paid to what others define as normal.

It was on my last home visit that I met the mother of five. Recently relocated from California and holding a Masters in Education. I found her conversation to be rather intriguing as she related to me a myriad of stories concerning the trials and tribulations, her husband and five children suffered prior to moving to Pittsburgh.

I empathized. How great the misfortune they must have had to endure to have made her pick up her family and leave sunny California to return to this cold, culturally barren wasteland better known as Pittsburgh.

I understood that she and her husband loved the idea of a big family and it became quite apparent after reading her case files and noting that she had five children all under the age of seven. It was unclear what the allegations were she and her husband were accused from but one thing was clear. They adored their children yet several neighbors had called in on the family.

Arriving a few doors down from her house with an intern from the University of Pittsburgh who couldn't have been more than nineteen or twenty at best. She accompanied me acting as my photographer as anything and everything had to be photographed and documented to aid in coming to a conclusion as to whether there really was an issue of neglect or abuse.

When I arrived there was quite the commotion coming from towards the back of the house. Fire trucks lined the driveway but I saw no smoke or anything that would suggest a fire. It was all a bit puzzling but I had a separate investigation; a county investigation to conduct to ascertain if there was either abuse or neglect involved in the household. My intern stayed close to my side as we passed several other agencies with pens and clipboards chattering away about this and that. Not knowing what all the commotion was about I was a little taken back although I did my best to remain professional.

Knocking at the back door a rather heavyset white woman with her hair pulled tightly back in a bun. Inviting us in a pungent smell met us once we were inside that was overwhelming. My young white intern pivoted quickly covering her nose and mouth before busting back out the back door leaving the screen door to bang loudly.

I understood as the lingering smell of cat urine had transformed itself into the smell of ammonia. I soon found myself quietly gasping for air and trying to keep my breakfast down at least until I'd completed my investigation. I stood in the kitchen and observed. The house seemed to be organized and in pretty good order except for on small detail. There were cats everywhere. In all, there were twenty six cats, five children and mom and dad in this tiny two bedroom home.

The smell itself was enough to call in a formal complaint but my client, this woman with her Masters in Education didn't and couldn't understand why someone would be so mean as to call Social Services to have her five children, (whom she truly loved and was devoted to), taken from her. To my client there was nothing wrong with maintaining a dwelling of this size with twenty-six cats and five children under the age of seven even if it meant she was unable to maintain both a safe and healthy environment.

Stepping outside following the interview for a breath of air and a smoke I was met by small groups of people from differing organizations each having their own agenda. I made my way over to the firemen. I saw no reason for their being there at all but then who was I to say? I'd always envisioned the brave fireman climbing up a tree to save some old woman's cat but twenty six?

"So what we lookin' at Tommy Boy?" A stout man on the cusp of middle age said to an older gentleman I gathered to be his supervisor.

"I don't think there's any doubt. It's gotta come down. The wear and tear done on that place by the cats and their lack of upkeep give me little choice but to condemn that hell hole."

So that was it. Minutes later back at my desk I got a call from the woman. Devastated. The house, her home had been condemned and it looked as though the city under the fire departments recommendation condemned the house leaving her homeless. And that was the good news.

I had the unenviable task of informing her that if she didn't make a major life change chances were good that she would not only lose her home but her children as well.

After filing my report all in attendance were in agreement that the family must move and all but one of the cats had to go. There was a social service agency which was going to be in attendance three days a week to insure that proper hygiene was instilled, and to make sure that maintenance of the household was kept up. Either that or I would be forced to take her children and place them in foster care.

On my second visit to inspect the home I stopped in to see my client and what efforts she'd made on her part. I impressed on her that she be adamant about abiding by the guidelines if she wanted to keep her family intact. Either that or I would be forced to put her children in a healthy more suitable environment.

It was then that that the flood gates opened. Tears flowed down the woman's face and I watched her age right before me.

"I'm trying so hard Mr. Brown. Please don't take my children away from me."

"Those are not my attentions Mrs. Kowinsky. My first priority is to make sure you provide a safe and healthy environment for your kids."

"I'm doing my best Mr. Brown. You see I spent the morning scrubbing and waxing all the floors."

I had to wonder if she were serious. She had be able to see that the floor shining was not a direct result of Mop-N-Glow but was the result of cat piss. Did she not understand that the yellow fly tape which now hung black from flies needed to be changed. And despite her pleading with me to believe that the hardwood floors were shining she was really trying and had waxed them for my visit I somehow found that hard to believe especially since it smelled the same way it did on my initial home visit. I had to take pictures to document my findings since no pictures had been taken on my prior visit.

Heading up the narrow staircase I was careful not to touch anything for fear of catching something and as I reached the top of the landing my client warned me that it

may be sticky underfoot as one of her children had spilled chocolate and hadn't had a chance to clean it up. And then I hit the landing where I quickly came to the realization that what she saw as chocolate on her top landing was a litter box without the kitty litter. There were feces everywhere.

This woman saw nothing wrong with having twenty-six cats and five children under the age of seven scampering around in such an unsavory, unsanitary environment. To her this was normal. The myriad of social agencies that milled around outside the house on my initial visit discussing the horrendous conditions that existed within the house went virtually unnoticed by my client. To her this was normal. If I had to garner a reason for her behavior I would have to say that my client had either grown up in a similar environment or had somehow become so tolerant that this lifestyle had become mundane and routine. In essence, her perception had resulted in this new normalcy.

Shane

In the early 90's, I believe it was 1992, I grew weary of my son's mother and the employment situation in North Carolina and with little prodding I picked up and moved to Charleston, South Carolina. I fell in love with Charleston, (despite its rather sordid past), from the moment I arrived and it was anxious to find out what it had to offer but the first thing I needed was a job so that I could partake in all of its treasures. I found myself working in a lock down facility for teenage sexual offenders. It is at this time that I would like to take pause and speak for a minute on a subject I probably shouldn't delve into no matter how gingerly and delicately I approach the subject.

My theory can and may be challenged and debated easily as I have no foundation or real knowledge in clinical or child psychology per se. However, I will hold to my theory that all behavior is learned and usually emanates from the home. I have come to this conclusion based on my fifteen years or so as a Special Education teacher whose specialization was in working with children and young adults with emotional and behavioral problems. And after such an experience it has become my unwavering contention that in more cases than not when behavior is initially learned it almost always emanates from the home. So, I contend that if that particular child has a behavior problem which in turn prevents that child from growing up to be a productive member of the society at large and he or she winds up under my tutelage it is usually through some fault or negligence by his caretakers. That being me said let me introduce you to Shane.

Shane was a fourteen year old white male who stood no more than four foot seven or eight. He was the smallest boy on the unit but what Shane lacked in physical stature he made up for in mouth and motion. From the time he woke up in the morning 'til I screamed lights out at night Shane was in the middle of something.

You see Shane grew up in the backwoods of West Virginia. Now understand that I have a penchant for those things that I don't rightly understand and cultures that are unique and different and the backwoods people of Pennsylvania, Kentucky, Tennessee and West Virginia that made the Appalachian mountains their home always intrigued me.

Yes, I've always been intrigued by the mountains, the stills, and the hillbilly culture. Yes, I like it right fine from my vantage point on 125th and Lenox up in Harlem. However, over the last five years or so I've had the occasion to take Amtrak from Pittsburgh to Washington D.C. on several occasions and on these occasions I prayed in earnest that the train would not suffer engine trouble or any other mechanical malfunction. I prayed that I would not be left at the mercy of these people in this God forsaken land with these people who incorporated the mean hateful spirit of America that was West Virginia. There was still that intrigue and I was not opposed to watching as many documentaries as I could in hopes of burying my own stereotypes and learning more about a culture so different than my own.

Enter Shane who immediately erased almost all of my homegrown stereotypes. Now I made it a point to not read a client's case file prior to meeting a client so as not to prejudge and enabling me to study and draw conclusions on my own thus giving them the opportunity to change and to reinvent themselves. This I hoped they would do in correcting whatever it was that required them to be in my custody.

This was understood that this was the way in which I handled my clients and as I had been successful no one questioned my methods. Well, that was up until Shane arrived when my supervisor insisted rather emphatically on me reading Shane's file so I could better understand this young boy and the cross he would bear all his life and the havoc he would cause through no fault of his own. From the file Shane had been neglected and abused more than any child I have ever come in contact with. From the file I gathered that Shane had been abandoned by his parents at an early age. His uncles took custody of Shane following his parents departure. With no employment and no income to speak of they resorted to making and selling moonshine. Fans of their own industry Shane reported during his initial intake interview that his uncles would more often than not drink more than they sold. When they were finished they would take turns having Shane perform fellatio on them. By the time he was thirteen Shane felt no certain way about it saying that this is all he had ever known. To Shane this was as normal and commonplace as waking up every morning. And he would gladly do it if it kept his uncles happy and kept them from beating him which they tended to do when they got too drunk. And like that Shane became apart of our unit. But if there was a heart wrenching scream or a threat made in earnest you could almost bet that Shane was somewhere in the mix.

Overall the unit was quiet with most of my clients focusing on personal goals that would hasten their release. But not Shane. To Shane this place with three meals a day and the camaraderie of the other boys must have made Shane feel he was in the Plaza Hotel and he had no intention of working on his goals. You see there was nothing wrong with him.

I found it ironic that in a place where all manner of deviancy were prevalent there still existed a code of ethics among these young men, an unstated law existed stating that they were all confined to this facility against their wishes but they were all going to prove to the world that a mistake had been made. And for some there was some basis to their argument. All that is except Shane who saw no reason for his being there since he had done nothing wrong.

I had one young man who had been taking liberties with his girlfriend of four years. They were the same age save a couple of months. Now he had turned eighteen while she was still seventeen and had been charged with statutory rape and remanded to us by the state for the next six months.

In any case, there was honor among thieves. Well, there was honor among everyone except Shane who had no boundaries and no sense. If you've ever watched the Andy Griffith Show and are familiar with Ernest T. Bass then you should get a good depiction of Shane.

I don't really think any of us took Shane too seriously. For the most part we simply monitored him making sure he didn't cause harm to himself or others. He'd write notes in his encrypted ledger and pass them to people he was fond of asking them to be his friend. In the note he'd promise fellatio that night if they promised to be his friend. To Shane this was the currency that made things happen.

The other boys would bring the notes to me. Ten minutes later I'd confront Shane who denied having written anything before giving me his word that it wouldn't happen again.

Not long afterwards, however I heard a loud, gut wrenching scream.

'Motherfucker, I gave you a pass earlier and you gonna come back and try me again. You must have a death wish motherfucker.'

Flicking on the light in the unit I noticed only one person standing. That person being six foot four, two hundred and eighty five pond, all-state defensive tackle Marcus Flowers. Standing over Shane who was curled up in the fetal position. Marcus kicked Shane savagely. I called for backup and two of my co-workers appeared.

'Marcus. Stop. Marcus,' but my pleas went unnoticed. He was in that zone and I knew he had long since grown past the idea of forgiveness and he would not be cognizant of death until after he had killed him and would regret it the rest of his life. At the time we were coordinated enough to rush him Marcus had just about worn out his size twelve Timberlands on Shane's ribs and chest. Shane was already unconscious and the way he was gasping for air I was pretty sure one or more of his ribs had been broken and a lung punctured as well.

But right now it was more important to calm Marcus' happy feet down which were intent on continuing to tune Shane up. I could understand Marcus' anger especially after rebuking Shane earlier that evening. Seems Shane knew no other way of fostering a friendship than the feeble social skills picked up in the backwoods of West Virginia's Appalachian Mountains which held to a different set of laws than the rest of the nation. It was these mores or laws or the lack thereof that had Shane gasping for life as the team of EMS workers placed Shane in the ambulance.

The blank look in Shane's eyes said everything and yet they said nothing. In his eyes he had done nothing but attempt to make his friend happy. After all, hadn't it gotten rid of his uncle's meanness and and brought a smile to their otherwise glum existence?

Shane's perception, his reality hadn't gotten him anything but two or three broken ribs and a punctured lung. The problem as I saw it was that through our perceptions based on our very own, unique experiences we create our own reality. And often times the reality is so askew from society at large that it draws attention yet none of us are in direct accord with the idea of normalcy.

Often times the reality is so far askew from the mainstream that it sends up red flags. In the case of Shane and my client with the cats the greater communities reaction to what they deemed abnormal brought an unequivocal reaction to what my clients deemed perfectly normal.

So, what is normal? My thesis simply contends that there is no normal. Sure there are certain mores, norms and laws that we adhere to in hopes of conforming to the norms of societal restraints placed on all of us. But alas we are the culmination of our lives and experiences up to and including that particular point in time. All that we have

witnessed in our lives and the way in which it affected our lives results in who we are today.

The soldier who has witnessed death firsthand is not the same man he was before he saw or took part in the killing(s). He cannot be. The value he initially placed on human life has either increased or decreased but there is one constant. And that is that we can assume that these actions will have a profound affect on the rest of his life.

Chances are his flirtation with so-called normalcy has ceased to exist as we know it. The clinical terms often associated with this are Post Traumatic Stress Syndrome and not to downplay the severity of the condition in any way but again it is my contention that there are a host of events that take place in most of our lives that can trigger the same response and in many if not most cases they go unnoticed.

I have read enough case files and encountered enough people who have been afflicted by life's travails to know that mental illness treated or untreated is still mental illness. Normalcy amongst far too many of us is but a mere perception and mental illness is far too rampant among far too many of us who give off the outward impressions that we are somehow normal.

Let me digress for a minute and share an example or two to illustrate my point.

Sadie Hopkins

Before I even begin to paint you a picture of Sadie let me start by setting the stage and letting you know where I saw myself at this particular juncture in my own journey.

I wasn't married but was cohabitating with the mother of my four year old son Christopher. I had no inclination to marry my child's mother but it had been instilled in me from the role my parents played in my life that both parents were needed to raise a happy well-balanced child. And though we'd only started dating a year or so before the next thing I knew she was pregnant. When I went to my father for advice and told him that Cheryl was pregnant he looked at me in no uncertain terms and simply said, 'well you know what you have to do'. I don't know what else he could have said. He was an honorable and righteous man so I listened and tried to adopt his constitution on life but the best I could do was to be there for my son. His mother and I had little in common aside from getting intoxicated and sleeping together but here I was doing the right thing, (or so I thought I was), but I was extremely troubled by these circumstances.

With no other alternative I committed to doing something to alleviate the situation. I worked. I worked all the time but not just to provide for my son. I had lofty goals and dreams and felt that with hard work I could achieve it all.

And so I worked and then I worked some more. I taught Special Education to middle schoolers with emotional and behavioral problems which in essence meant I taught little Black boys and girls that other teachers decided they didn't want in their classrooms. When I was finished there I went downtown and worked as a short order cook and dishwasher in my parents restaurant. At night when I got home I worked on my weekly sports column and acted as sports editor for the local Black newspaper. On

Wednesdays I drove the newspaper up to Laurinburg and waited for it to be printed before bringing it back to the office. On the weekends I worked another full time job taking care of the mentally handicapped at a group home.

I was doing well to say the least. Well, financially that is... And to the victor go the spoils and so I went out and bought the hottest red,BMW on the market. Now it was hard to tell me anything but after a week or two the novelty wore off and it became little more than just another rather expensive monthly bill. A month later I purchased a town house walking distance from the mall and I thought I had arrived. But it did nothing to fill the emptiness I felt inside. I knew that material rewards could not fulfill the void in me. I knew what was missing, what I needed to complete me.

What my life was lacking was a significant other, a soul-mate and since I saw none on the immediate horizon I continued to busy myself with work and the hard work paid off with me garnering praise both at school and the group home.

I was thirty-five and determined to be retired by the time I was forty. It was a realistic goal and certainly within reason if I just stayed the course. At the time a woman, a relationship would have been nice to wile away the few hours I reserved for myself each

evening but since I saw no prospects in the foreseeable future I continued my maniacal trek towards financial security although I had no plan. I just worked hard.

I was always racing from one late appointment to the next and it just so happened that this happened on one of these days when I pulled up at the YWCA Day Care Nursery, double parking and running in to get my son. I just prayed he wasn't the last one there. I didn't want to be the one responsible for keeping the day care staff from their families but most of all I didn't want my son Christopher to even entertain the idea that he'd been forgotten.

As I arrived he ran to me elated about seeing his dad and ready to tell all about his day. I apologized and thanked his teacher, an elderly, statuesque, Black woman by the name of Ms. Cohill for loving him like he were her own.

'Never a problem... You know Chris is my buddy,' the tall, sixtyish, woman said smiling before sweeping Chris up in a bear hug and showering his face and neck with kisses. Chris giggled and struggled trying to escape her clutches but it was no use. She had him. When she finally put him down she turned and faced me.

'You know I have my grandson Jalil for the weekend. It would be nice if Chris could come spend the weekend.'

'That sounds really good Ms. Cohill. Lord knows I could use a break but let me check with his mom and make sure she doesn't have anything planned for him. I'll let you know tomorrow if that's okay.'

'That's fine. You have a wonderful night Mr. Brown. Bye Chris,' she said waving to Chris.

Grabbing Chris in my arms I picked up where Ms. Cohill left off smothering him with kisses. He wiggled, laughing uncontrollably. His laughter was infectious and made an otherwise unbearable day bearable.

Letting the screen door of the old wooden house bang loudly behind me I heard someone yell.

'Ms. Cohill is that Mr. Brown?'

'Yes it is.'

'Would you stop him for a minute. I'd like to speak to him.'

Ms. Cohill didn't have to repeat a word. I'd heard it all. I stepped back into the vestibule as a light mist began to fall.

'Mr. Brown,' she said grinning as she came down the stairs from her office.

'Ms. Hopkins. As usual you're looking quite nice. Tell me that's not cashmere?' I said touching the bottom of her sweater.

'Stop that,' she said pulling away and exhibiting a slight lisp. Donning a plain white ruffled blouse, plaid skirt which fell right below the knee, with a pair of burgundy penny loafers that gave her the appearance of a school marm more than a director. But if there was one thing about Ms. Hopkins that impressed me above all else it was the fact that she just exuded class.

Well schooled she'd received her Bachelor's Degree from Bennet, the very prestigious, historically Black all girls college. I'd be selling her short if I were to attribute all her professionalism and quiet reserve to Bennet as I did not know her before then. Still, the only other person I knew that attended the school possessed all the same qualities.

'You said you needed to speak to me?'

'Yes. It wasn't really important. I was just curious about a few things.'

'Such as?'

'Like I said it wasn't important.'

'It was important enough for you to have Ms. Cohill stop me.'

'I just wanted to know if you go to church.'

I smiled now knowing that she really didn't need anything.

'I'm not sure what you're asking me but yes I have been to church.'

Now she was smiling.

'No silly. You know what I'm asking you.'

'No. I'm not sure that I do.'

'What I'm asking is if you attend on a regular basis?'

'No. I can't say that I do but again I don' think that's what you really want to know. I think what you're really trying to ask me is if I belong to any certain church.

And to that I would say no. That would make me religious. I think I am more spiritual than religious,' I answered giving her pause for thought.

It was beginning to rain harder and the misting had turned into a steady drizzle.

'And what is that supposed to mean?' It just sounds like you're afraid to commit, like you're running from commitment. Just like with Chris' mother. You need to go ahead and commit to both God and that baby's mama.'

I smiled but was seething inside. I have never understood why women chose to cast judgment on men as if they alone had been up the mountain and witnessed the burning bush. Still, I smiled. Perhaps it was no more than a way to start a

conversation and so I took her comments with a grain of salt and began to tease her in turn.

'Seriously though. You need to go ahead and commit to that baby's mother.'

'And why would I do that Ms. Hopkins? Then I would miss out on making you the next Mrs. Brown. I said buckling Christopher in his car seat before turning to face her.

'Shoot. You'd be attending church on the regular if you ever had plans on seeing me,' she said rather emphatically.

'I wish you'd said something sooner. I would have been in church. But now that I know that's one of the requirements what time shall I pick you up on Sunday?'

This woman always so calm and reserved blushed deeply.

'You're not serious.'

'As a heart attack. Now give me your address and phone number so I know where to pick you up from and can call when I'm on my way. But let's continue this over lunch tomorrow. My parents are probably wondering where I am. My treat. I know this cute little restaurant that's walking distance from here and it might not hurt you to jog over there,' I said looking her up and down.

'I'm just saying it looks like you've put on a pound or two since I last saw you. Don't take it the wrong way. You still look fine as hell to me even with the extra weight.'

Sadie smiled broadly.

'Go to hell Mr. Brown.'

'So that's what they teach you at your church. I'm not sure I want to go now,' I joked. 'Seriously though do you like good soul food?'

'Love it.'

'Then its a date then. Say three o'clock?'

'I suppose. Would you like me to bring Chris when I come? That way you won't have to make two trips?'

'I'd appreciate that.'

'Okay. Well then I guess I'll talk to you tomorrow.'

'Not if I can talk to you tonight,' I said handing handing her my card. 'If you find a few minutes give me a call. I should be home by eight, eight-thirty.'

'I'll give it some thought,' she said smiling as she walked away.

Watching her walk away I thanked God for creating Sadie Hopkins and her chocolate frame.

At a little after eight the phone rang.

'You busy?'

'Never too busy for you my love.'

'Good answer Mr. Brown. Good answer. You are always so cool and self assured about everything that I don't know whether or not to believe you half the time. I don't know whether you're selling me a line or not. But anyway moving right along what do you have planned for this evening?'

'Could be so what I suggest you do is take your time, feel me out and see what happens, see how it feels. Then take a step back and ask yourself where you want it to go. If it doesn't feel right then just walk away. In the end we will always be friends.'

'Oh, you don't know how I hate you right now,' Sadie laughed. 'If it were just that easy. That's always been the way I approach things but in the process of getting to know someone you develop feelings and it's always harder to walk away. Besides that you're basically married. You know now I think about it I've got to be crazy to even entertain the thought of you. Let me go. Have a good night Mr. Brown.'

'You too Sadie. I'll see you tomorrow.'

'We'll see.'

I couldn't argue with her. I knew she was right. Chris' mom loved me but I had promises and obligations. Still, I knew and understood Sadie's feelings. It was a no win situation for her and yet I had no intention of walking back my feelings where she was concerned. The next day I played my hole card.

'I was hoping you would come.'

'Only because I told you I would bring Chris but then you were counting on that weren't you?'

I smiled.

'I believe it was you that made the arrangements but I hope that isn't the only reason I'm you seeing today. Sit down. Have you eaten?' Before she could answer I was gone and back with a Mason jar filled with ice cold lemonade and a half a slab of baby back ribs, macaroni and cheese, some collards, a slice of cornbread and and a bowl of homemade peach cobbler with two scoops of vanilla ice cream.

'My God! Mr. Brown what are you trying to do to me. Just yesterday you were commenting on me gaining weight and now this,' she said surveying the table. 'Messing with you, I'll be big as a house.'

'And you'll still be the best looking girl at the ball?'

'Ahh... Despite all the drama I can understand why the women are so crazy now about you,' she blushed.

'Don't know who all these women you're referring to are and it really doesn't matter. There is only one woman I have my sights set on and that woman happens to be you.'

It was obvious that she felt uncomfortable accepting compliments. She immediately changed the subject.

'Oh my God! These ribs are simply divine. Does Mrs. Brown cook like this everyday?'

"For as long as I can remember. And if you tell her that, trust me, you've made a friend for life.'

'Just as soon as I finish if I can finish all this food.'

'Not to brag but you have to be there for one of her Saturday morning breakfasts. They're to die for. Homemade biscuits and baked apples along with bacon, sausage or ham. I kid you not.'

'Sounds absolutely wonderful. When you going to invite me?'

'Sorry it's a members only thing designated for family and family only. But don't worry when we get married you'll be a regular member.'

'Don't you think you're moving kind of fast for a man with a live in woman?'

'Okay enough with the whole wife thing. Trust me I gave the whole situation considerable thought when we got off the phone last night and I agree that it would be difficult for us to move forward in any way, shape or form until I dissolve this relationship with my son's mother but I think a good first step would be for us to start

searching for an apartment and put some distance between us. It's something I probably should have done years ago.'

'Whoa! Slow your roll! Don't you think you're jumping the gun just a little Romeo? I think you may have the wrong lady. In case you didn't know and how could you but I will never share a man's house until I am legally wed.'

'Then perhaps we should get married on Monday and get the apartment on Tuesday.

Looking back I'm glad she was a little more grounded than I was. So desperate for a good strong, bright sista that if she had agreed chances are I would have probably been married.

'Lord why me?' she laughed. 'You're crazy. You know that don't you?'

'I've been told that on occasion but I don't put a whole lotta thought in other peoples opinions. Can't do that and keep up with my own. You feel me?'

'I do.'

'Listen sweetheart I've got to go in and knock these dishes out or I'll end up being here half the night and I still have to go home and grade papers. But listen I'll be at the group home tonight. Why don't you stop by after ten? My residents should be sleep by then and the staff quarters are separate from the rest of the house so we should have some privacy.'

'Really. What it is are you not getting? Didn't I just tell you that ain't nothing happening until I'm legally married.'

'Please tell me why it is that your brain continually retreats to sex whenever there's talk of a man and a woman being alone together. Could you please explain that to me.'

'The problem is not any man or woman. The problem is you and I. I can feel your eyes on me when I'm walking away. I know you want me right now,' she said sliding her foot up my leg. 'Leave you and I somewhere alone and someone's liable to get raped. And it might just be you,' she smiled.

I had to laugh.

'Wow! You've got some imagination. And the whole time I was thinking popcorn and a movie.'

'I'm sure.'

'So, I'll see you tonight?'

'If you promise it's just for popcorn and a movie.'

'Scouts honor.'

The residents were all sound asleep when I heard her car pull up at the side door. For the first time since I'd known her I was uneasy, even a little nervous although for the life of me I didn't know why though I had my suspicions. Perhaps she was right. Our passions had been pent up up for far too long. We were both ready to take the next step. At least I was.

Sadie, on the other hand, wrestled with the countless hurts that preceded my arrival wondering if her new found religion could truly replace man's physical presence. Her new religion spoke of discipline, restraint, and delayed gratification. She accepted this in lieu of her last relationship which had been so traumatic that she had dismissed the notion of men altogether and supplanted it with the one man she knew would not hurt her and that was the Lord Jesus Christ.

Sad thing was that she wasn't the only one wrestling with demons. I wrestled with demons of my own. I wanted her and only her although I had no idea why she appealed to me so.

Arriving at the side door I promptly ushered her into the tiny, staff bedroom. I sat on the bed the only piece of furniture in the room other than a nightstand.

Sadie stood before me in a floral robe and those huge curlers you see old white women wearing in those fifties movies. This was not the oh so prim and reserved

Ms. Hopkins I'd come to know. Sitting next to me I wondered if this was her way of offering herself to me. Lord knows enough time had passed. When our hands touched I knew it was time. Still, in not wanting to seem too forward I waited for her to touch me again before I turned and kissed her deeply, passionately as my fingers toyed with the buttons on her pajamas until I reached her ripe but petite breasts. When I heard her breathing deeply and felt no resistance I continued my downward journey. She was moaning now and I grew in confidence knowing that with gentle patience we would soon be intimate.

And then as if a starter gun had gone off she jumped out of my arms and was out the door. Gone.

Stunned I sat on the edge of the bed and wondered what had gone wrong. Had I done something? Could it be those demons again? I struggled to understand but it was beyond me. Who could possibly know what another person's thinking and especially a woman. All I knew at the time was that she completed me. She fulfilled my every desire and I wanted nothing more than to consummate our relationship with intimacy.

Marriage was definitely on the horizon. I wanted all of her, mind, body and soul.

Each time we seemed to be getting closer she would do something to sabotage my

efforts in a vain attempt to push me away. I didn't understand. It was obvious that

she liked me, maybe even loved me at this point so why wouldn't she allow it to

come to fruition and bask in the warm rays of love. What was she afraid of?

I was tucked away deep in thought when the phone rang.

'Hello.'

'Oh Bert sweetheart I am so sorry. Please don't be angry with me. I told you I had

some issues coming into this this. I guess I'm just having a hard time dealing with

how fast everything is moving. You know I'm crazy about you but it's like

sometimes I have to pinch myself to make sure this is real and not a dream. I'm

just afraid that one day you're going to wake up and say it's over. I'll be crushed

and cursing myself for wearing my heart on my sleeve. I guess what it all comes

down to is that I just don't want to be hurt again.'

'That's understandable. I'm glad you called. The way you left I thought you'd

had a sudden epiphany that said 'he's not the one for me' and just left.

'And to think I thought you were the one with all the confidence.'

I was angry and perhaps a bit discouraged. After all, I'd shown her the best of what I had to offer baring my heart and soul and with this latest rebuff I knew that I was somehow still lacking. My ego was in a sad state.

By now we both come to accept that she was my woman and if she accepted that how could she possibly question my intentions.

'I can question them because no matter how sincere you profess to be I've stated my intentions to more than one man and they've all lent an ear and listened and

agreed in principle to honor my wishes right up until we had sex. And if you hadn't noticed I came to you single and unattached. I'm sorry sweetheart but I need to be sure this time. I'm tired of crying myself to sleep every time a brotha walks out the door with my heart in his hands. Yes, I question your intentions. When we first started talking you assured me that you had no skeletons in the closet. Do you recall that? That's what you told me and I so wanted to believe you that I did. Then Edna popped up out of the blue. You never mentioned her.'

'What was to mention?'

'How about the fact that she's in love with you.'

'In love with me? Am I missing something? Is there something that you know that I don't know?'

'Call it a woman's intuition. Call it whatever you like but I'm telling you just from her behavior that she's obsessed with you Bert. I can' blame her and don't blame her. That's not my concern. My concern is that you told me that there were no skeletons in the closet.'

'You're right.'

'I know I'm right and I also know that you slept with her.'

'More women's intuition I suppose.'

I was shocked she was taking this route to mask her own insecurites and shortcomings.

'You slept with her didn't you?'

'Come on Sadie. Where's this coming from?'

'Tell me. Did you sleep with her?'

'Long before I met you.'

'And did you promise her the same thing you promised me when you were trying to get in her pants?'

'It wasn't like that at all sweetheart.'

'Oh no? Well then, tell me how it was.'

'I'm telling you it wasn't like that at all. She was my trainer when I first started working at the group home and after shadowing her for more than a week she left and came back, let herself in the staff quarters, climbed into the bed with me and well you know the rest.'

'And it never occurred to you to just say no?'

'In all honesty 'no' that never crossed my mind.'

'Oh no? Well, at least you're being honest. More affirmation that all men are dogs.'

'A woman comes to my bedroom door and climbs into my bed and I'm a dog for accepting her in. Wow.'

'Yes. If you don't mind me asking me what was the trigger in her case?'

'I don't follow. What do you mean what was the trigger?'

'Well, you keep telling me that what attracts you to me is my intellect. What was your attraction to Edna?'

'I can't even begin to compare the two.'

'Try.'

'Well, in your case I was and am pursuing a long and fulfilling relationship. I think I've been both patient, caring and understanding. How long have we been together. Three or four months by my calculations and we still haven't had sex. So, I'm not sure what kind of comparison you want me to draw.'

'Let's just say I'm curious as to what made you sleep with her.'

'Like I said there was no rhyme or reason. She came to me in a silk negligee, opened it wide, revealing herself and I took her or she took me and we blended for a brief moment in time and that was basically the extent of it.'

'Oh hell no. I know you're not trying to tell me you slept with her one time and she fell in love and became obsessed with you. I know that you don't expect me to believe that was the extent of it.'

'Okay. Pause. Please explain to me why the sudden interest in Edna? I know the director of the YMCA Day Care nurse isn't threatened by a lil' ol' country girl.'

'Jealous? Don't make me laugh. That's ludicrous and let me tell you what else is ludicrous. When I leave your house like I did last night and this lil' ol'country girl is outside waiting for me and follows me halfway home blowing her horn and shouting obscenities at me.'

'No she didn't,' I said shocked by this latest news.

'Oh but she did. Now be honest with me. How many times did you sleep with her? Did you two have a relationship? What promises did you make to her to have her act this way.'

I sat numb trying to process what I'd just heard. I'd seen Edna on occasion sitting pensively outside the townhouse but that had been months ago. Prior to that we'd slept together on occasion at her place out in the country and I enjoyed her company but she was by no means what I sought for myself over the long haul. What she was at the time was good company. What Edna was was fun. She was barbecues and baseball games. It was racing her in my BMW and she in her 240Z on North Carolina's back roads. At night after drinking and too tired to drive home I'd crawl in bed next to her and call it a night. Sometimes we'd have sex but most nights we were too exhausted to do anything but sleep.

One day my supervisor, a very classy, middle-aged white woman pulled me aside. My mother had done a feature article on her and my work and work ethic had me at the top of her list for model employees. I respected her so when she took me aside to warn me about Edna I should have paid closer attention as I believed she had my best interest at heart. I also think being the director of a mental health facility she may have had a bit more insight into what ailed Edna. What I think her real concern though was my welfare.

'Other than the obvious why are you dating her?'

There was little doubt that she was physically attractive. And she was more than competent in the bedroom. But there were definitely issues boiling right below the surface. I'd seen her break into a white hot heat when someone said something that she was offended by or something she didn't feel was right. I'd seen the anger, the explosions but as of yet they had not been directed at me.

My supervisor warned me.

'You be careful. I don't know if you know it or not but Edna's a loose cannon.'

I ignored this advice in large part since I had no plans on going any further than where we were now. We were friends who enjoyed each other's company. That was it. Or so I though until Sadie recounted the events of the night before.

Then again that's not necessarily true. Now that I think back I do remember one Friday we bumped into each other at the office picking up our paychecks. We hadn't seen or talked to each other in weeks and I just figured she was busy and I certainly was so... I still considered us friends.

'You going to cash your check?'

'Yes ma'am,' I answered.

I was actually glad to see her. I welcomed her company and catching up on what I missed. That's what I hoped for. But on this day I got a whole lot more than I'd bargained for. Being a Friday the lines at the drive thru teller were much longer than usual giving Edna's anger time to reach the boiling point. It started off innocent enough.

'Mind if I ask you a question?'

'Sure sweetheart. Ask me anything,' I said almost sorry before the words left my lips.

'How is it that for months we talked and saw each other almost everyday and then just like that I don't hear or see from you at all. Not even a call to see how I'm doing. Did I offend you in some way?'

'No, Edna.'

'Then why? What happened? I thought we had something special.' I could see her eyes welling with tears.

'I don't know. I guess there comes a time when you have to take a step back to see where you're headed. When I took a step back I didn't like what I saw. I didn't like the person I was becoming and I had lost focus so I took time out to reassess my life and try to get things back on track.'

'I completely understand but don't you think that when you're in a relationship you owe it to your partner to let them know when you plan to fall off the edge of the earth never to be heard from again?'

'To be honest with you I didn't know I was in a relationship. I thought we were just two friends who liked to kick it every now and then.'

'Excuse me. I don't know what you mean by kickin' it but if you haven't noticed I ain't one of these ho's that goes around kickin' it with friends. That's not who I am. I thought you knew me better than that. I fell in love with you and that's the only reason I let you have your way. Before you it had been seven years.'

Before I could continue let me inform you that it wasn't unusual for Edna and the Burns to carry firearms. These were just the sort of down home southern folks that had their own kind of backyard justice. And Edna was if nothing else a Burns.

'How can you love me one day and not know me the next? I mean who does that? And I know you love me. You can't tell me you don't. You told me you did when we made love. I know you love me.' The tears were flowing now and her eyes had gotten glassy and glazed. I knew the Edna I knew was no longer there.

Pulling the sawed off shotgun from between her legs and leveling it at my chest she screamed.

'Tell me you love me.'

I was suddenly very calm. And for some reason I no longer seemed in control of my faculties. I heard a voice but could not distinguish its origin. I wanted to tell her anything that would assure my safety but what I heard come from my mouth was quite different.

'I will not tell you that I am or was ever in love with you. I like you but there is more to me than drinking and getting high. I see other things for myself. I have goals and dreams that are different from yours. I want to go fishing off the pier down at Carolina Beach. I want to have a tiny bungalow right there on the beach with nothing but a radio and a stove. It'll have a porch and rocking chair and this is where I'll wile the years away alone if need be.

In the winter when all is deserted I will hunker down at my desk by the fireplace and write the next great novel .

This is my dream. I want to read and write and be in contact with people that share these same pursuits so that I may learn vicariously. You see I am curious as to what is out there in the great beyond. And then I stopped and asked myself what I was doing to make my dreams come to fruition. The drinking, getting high and laying up with a woman who wants nothing more than to lay up was not getting me any closer to realizing my dream.'

When I finished she lowered the shotgun and let her head fall to her chest. Again the tears flowed freely.

"And the whole time I thought it was another woman. Now I almost wish it had been another woman. I could have at least fought that but how can I fight you pursuing a dream? Funny thing though. The whole time I was falling in love I knew that I wouldn't be able to keep you. I used to fantasize my own little fairy tale where the big time New York City boy falls in love with the lil country girl. It ends where the big city boy buys the lil country gal a house in the country where they raise their seven children in heavenly bliss.'

'It sounds wonderful and who knows maybe we can revisit this in a few years. Right now I need to pursue a few things so that I can one day afford that little house in the country.'

All was relatively peaceful on the ride back to the office.

'Thanks for the ride Edna.'

'No problem,' she said almost as if nothing had transpired as she searched her purse for her lipstick. 'You'll be hearing from me. I know you don't think Edna Burns gives up that easily when she sets her sights on something she wants,' she said leaning over and pulling the too short dress down over her thick caramel thighs.

It was at this time that I concluded two things where Edna Burns was concerned. She was fine as hell and as looney as any woman I've come to know. I also came to this conclusion. I would definitely lose this gun totin' lunatic's number before she saw a reason to put an end to me. Up until Sadie brought me news of Edna's return I hadn't seen her in months.

Now this.

"Yeah this ol' crazy heifer started screaming and yelling obscenities as soon as I walked out the door. She kept saying that I better stay away from her f-in man. I wanted to ask her if her man knew that he belonged to her but I kept it moving. At first I kept turning around to see who she was talking to. It took me awhile to realize who she was talking to. I just got in my car and left then the next thing I know is someone's flashing their brights at me trying to get me to pull over.'

'Are you serious?'

'That's when I said this girl's dangerous. I was headed home and then I thought about this crazy chick following me. I mean every time I stopped at a light she would pull up and start telling me how she was going to f*** me up.'

'So what did you end up doing?'

'I drove downtown to the police station and walked in and took out a complaint and a restraining order. Seems this isn't the first time she's been in trouble with the law.'

'That was smart but I'm still having a hard time trying to understand why she would follow you in the first place.'

'We don't know how long she was sitting outside but if she saw me going in with the wine that would be provocation enough for that crazy chick. You must have really whipped that thang on her. Makes me wonder about you Mr. Brown.'

'I didn't know. You have to believe me. When you asked me if I had any skeletons I didn't know she would enter into the equation. We had a minute and then went our separate ways. Or so I thought.'

'Well, you thought wrong. She still considers you to be her man. That girl's got some serious issues. You better be careful.'

'I think if anything it's a matter of perception. I was under the impression that we were just enjoying each other's company and that in itself was the extent of it.'

'That may have been the extent of it for you but a woman is a different sort of breed. A woman falls in love. A man falls in love with sex. So, while you were tappin' it on occasion she was planning her wedding with the man of her dreams.'

What could I say? I knew she was right.

'You still there?'

'Yeah I'm still here. and as usual you're correct in your prognosis. I am sorry though. I really didn't know it would come down to this.'

'Don't apologize to me. Apologize to her. It's her heart you ripped out.'

'I'll do that.'

'Once you do that give me a call. Oh, and while I have you I need you to do me a favor in the morning.'

'What's that? I'm afraid my slow leak stopped being a slow leak.'

'Is the tire completely flat?

'I'm afraid so. I was wondering if you could stop by in the morning and change it for me.'

Of course it would go flat on the coldest day of the year, I mumbled to myself. 'Listen mornings are rough on me with having to get Chris off and all. Why don't you put the key over the visor and I'll come by and change it now.'

'Are you sure?'

'Yes ma'am. Just put the key over the visor.'

'You're a doll. Whatever would I do without you? You are definitely carving out a niche in my heart. I may just have to keep you around awhile.'

'The thought is somewhat appealing although I don't know a man in his right mind that would even entertain the idea of entering into a relationship with a frigid woman.'

'Oh, no you didn't,' she said laughing heartily.

36'And Sadie.'

'Yes dear.'

'Didn't I ask you to put the key over the visor?'

'Yes dear.'

'Then why isn't they over the visor?'

'Oh, you're here. Wow. That was quick. Let me throw a robe on and I'll meet you at the door.'

Now North Carolina is not normally known for its cold weather but this winter had been unseasonably cold and not even the turtleneck and sweater did little to buffer me against the biting winds. The cold made it seem like eons before the front door of the old dilapidated brownstone opened. In a floral house robe and slippers Sadie

looked even sexier than I last remembered.

'Where's your roommate?'

'Her mom wasn't feeling well so she went home for a few days to be with her.'

'That's too bad,' I said sliding my hands under her robe and unhooking her bra.

'The tire Mr. Brown. The tire...' she repeated, grinning and pushing me away.

'Priorities Mr. Brown. If I hadn't called you I probably wouldn't have heard from

you. And if it weren't for my tire I know I wouldn't be looking at you now so let's

try and stay focused.'

I shot her a glance that made her cower. Taking the keys I braved the cold.

Fifteen minutes later I was finished and looked to return the keys. I found Sadie in

her bedroom dressed in a black negligee, black fishnet stockings and black heels

looking just as good as she wanted.

Moving closer I saw that she'd been crying. Her tear stained cheeks told it all

despite her trying to compose herself.

'Wanna talk about it sweetheart?'

Burying her head in my shoulder she let go. I don't know how long I held her but whatever it was that was bothering her was deep seated and longstanding. I agonized right along with her. I didn't want to see her in any pain. I never asked her what was wrong. I was sure in due time and when the time was right she would tell me everything.   Later that night the flood gates opened as Sadie recounted her childhood. When she finished I only wondered how she endured and come through as well as she had.

Seems there were five children born to a single mother. Sadie was herself a twin. She and her sister were the only ones that had the same father. The rest of her siblings had different fathers. It wasn't unusual for mom to fall head over heels with some man and go traipsing off with him abandoning her five children or shipping them off. One time she allowed one of her suitors to move in and he had beaten and sexually molested both Sadie and her sister.

Mom refused to acknowledge it even after she was confronted by her twins. It seemed that anytime there seemed some stability in the home mom would jump up, pack her bags and move in with this guy or that until he too grew tired of her at which time she would return home tail tucked between her legs.

And now after another long absence she'd call to update Sadie on her whereabouts and invite her to come stay with her in another last ditch effort to make amends for past transgressions. Poor Sadie was traumatized by the whole chain of events and had yet to get over it or come to grips with it. What struck me as peculiar was that at thirty-two Sadie was seriously considering moving back to her mother who was now in Charleston, South Carolina living in a tiny one bedroom apartment with the super of the apartment complex. So desperate for her mother's affection that I watched as she anguished for weeks hoping and praying that her mother wouldn't hurt her again.

I listened intently but said little. I don't think she needed any advice but simply needed someone to use as a sounding board. When she was finished I stood and kissed her gently on her forehead and said goodnight.

Grabbing my hand she pulled me back to the bedside looked deeply into my eyes before pleading.

'Please don't go. I don't want to be alone tonight.'

Now for the first time I had my druthers. After listening to all of the atrocities heaped upon she and her siblings I now understood why she had no trust in others. She would no longer commit for fear of being hurt.

'They've always left me. Nobody has ever really wanted to be with me. They always leave. Tell me you won't leave me bay. Promise me right now before you share my bed that you won't leave me for another woman,' she said tugging at my belt.

Again I had my reservations. At first I thought I recognized the same needs I found inherent in myself. I needed a soul mate, in my life; but to date I hadn't found anyone as bright and compatible as Sadie. And as much as we loved sex we did not spend a lot of time in the bedroom. Our love was spontaneous. We could be sitting in the car talking before going into the mall and the next thing you kew one of us had triggered something in the other and before you knew it we were tearing each other's clothes off.

At other times a quick glance where our eyes would meet would lead to us making love on the fold up cot in her office while staff and students bustled around downstairs.

Truth was that we were in love and things couldn't have been much better. We traveled constantly up and down the east coast pursuing my newest hobby at her insistence. She later inspired me into turning my hobby into a most lucrative business. And this is what I cherished about her. She was inspirational and motivational and had

my best interest at heart. She was just what the doctor ordered in my quest to be complete and at peace. If nothing else she was the stability I so badly needed in my life.

I heard NBA legend Bill Russell comment recently that after the life he's had here heaven would be a letdown. I concurred and then when I didn't think life could get much better the phone rang.

'Hey sweetie. How are you?'

'I'm better now that I'm talking to you. I've been trying to reach you all day.'

'I'm sorry bay. Mommy's had me tied up for most of the day. She's really going through it.'

'Anything I can help you with?'

'No. Same ol'. Same ol.' Family's at war again is all. Mommy's holding out an olive branch and trying to make amends but my brothers and sisters aren't having it.

Mommy's hurt and she asked me to come and stay with her awhile. I turned in my resignation this morning so I should be leaving in the next two weeks.'

Again I was shocked.

'Have you really thought about this? I mean have you really given this considerable thought?' I asked more hurt and dejected than anything. She hadn't given any thought as to how I felt about her leaving. The whole affair appeared very selfish but my pride refused to let her see just how hurt I was.

'I've thought about it far more than you'll know.'

'And what about us? You know you're breaking my heart.'

'You know for a long time I wasn't real sure where you stood but I've come to realize that you do love me but not enough to leave your son and to be perfectly honest with you I would look at you sideways if you got up and left your son for some woman. But the plain truth of it is that you won't leave Cheryl and I owe it to myself to be more than a sidepiece. So, I'm going to go babysit mommy while she babysits me. We don't really know each other but we do share one thing in common.'

'What's that?'

'Neither of us has much luck with men. Seems the ones I choose seem to always belong to someone else and I have a hard time sharing. I'm just not built like that.'

'So just like that we're over, finished?'

'That is entirely up to Mr. Brown. The balls in your court. You know the rules if you want me on your team.'

'So what you're saying is it's over?'

I knew I was being redundant but I was having a hard time processing. How could she just get up and leave me? But here she was doing just that.

In the next two weeks I begged and pleaded for her not to go. She was my mentor, business partner, best friend, conscious and lover. And she was about to leave me. In those last days I reconciled myself to the fact that Charleston was a mere three hour drive.

I still spoke to her everyday but I missed her presence, her infectious smile. I remembered how I made it a point to see her least once a day. Seeing her could turn gray overcast skies sunny and blue. The fact is I loved that woman and I missed her dearly.

'Then you know what you have to do Mr. Brown,' would be her response. I groaned. Sadie was steadfast in her all-or-nothing approach to our relationship. Finally, I gave in and made the three hour drive to be with my baby during which time I contemplated all that I was leaving and in the end it was all secondary to my love for this coffee colored woman.

Her mother and her boyfriend had a cute little one bedroom just big enough for two. I didn't mind though. I was back with Sadie. And that's all that mattered.

We slept on a twin sized rollout bed in the living room and no finer twin bed could be found. We made good love every night and slept like babies. The days we spent job hunting all over Charleston. Within the week I'd found employment at a local convenience store. A week later I also found employment as a habilitation specialist which was nothing more than a glorified caretaker for the mentally handicapped. The pay wasn't great but I picked up so much overtime that I came close to doubling my salary by years end.

Sadie was working in some capacity for the city and we quickly found ourselves in a position to find a place of our own. I was going to miss her mom and her boyfriend. They were simple, down home folks who exposed me to things unique to South Carolina's low country like scrimping and crabbing off the pier with a piece of string and a chicken neck.

Life was good. We were working hard and now were seeing the fruits of our labors. We soon had enough saved for an apartment of our own. Sadie was more than ready to go by this time. She was still having difficulty in her relationship with her mother. Frustrated by the fact that her mom would not acknowledge fact that she'd abandoned her children and put her twin daughters in precarious positions. Sadie was adamant about starting the healing process but it all started with her mother acknowledging that she'd contributed to the abuse and neglect of her children and this she would not do.

I had a whole 'nother take on the situation. From my viewpoint her mother had done everything she possibly could have to make our stay comfortable but the scars were deep and she had hardly begun to heal. I tried to talk to her, reason with her.

'Sweetheart your mother has more days in back of her than she does in front of her so why don't you let the past go. She has to deal with those issues and atone with them when she meets her God at the pearly gates. But as Christians we are supposed to embrace the sinful and show them a better way. Not be judge and jury and condemn them for past transgressions. How does the saying go? 'He who has not sinned cast the first stone.'

'No. No. No. Not this time. I don't care what kind of act she puts on she has never acknowledged what she did to us and I'm sorry but until she does I will never

forgive her. She has to stop living in denial. That's why her life is stagnant and she can't move forward and get on with life. And 'no' I can't let her off the hook. She needs to acknowledge what she did.'

She was usually more logical in her thinking than I was but not in this instance. I listened and empathized. I knew I did not have the answers. In her mind she'd given her last best effort to reconcile herself with her mother but for some reason was still not satisfied with their relationship.

I cared. I wanted to see her happy. If that meant us moving away from her mother and getting a place of our own I was all for it. We had yet to live together but I

saw little reason for it not to work. We were both pretty fair cooks, obsessive compulsive neat freaks and we enjoyed each other's company. Laughter between us came easily. I loved her and she was the first woman I ever made love to. Oh, I'd slept with countless others but she was the first woman that I both loved and had the opportunity to make love to. And it wasn't just good. It was incredible. Well, that was right up until we moved.

Like I said I am no psychiatrist but the results from her short stay with her mother only exacerbated the belief that her mother neither loved or wanted her. This was a recurring theme throughout her life and her stay only reaffirmed what she already believed. And that was okay. This was her issue and she was the only one that could resolve it. This was my way of handling it.

Sadie, on the other hand, seemed to have lost all sense of confidence and in doing so had somehow lost herself. To me it was almost as if she'd had a nervous breakdown. No longer was she the happy, carefree woman with all the spontaneity in the world. No longer did she make you feel alive just being in her presence. Nowadays she was no more than a a shell of herself.

I became the focal point of all that was wrong with her life and the recurring victim of her anger. She became disenchanted at work and found herself embroiled in a few minor scrapes that months prior she would have avoided like the plague. The few friends we had come to accrue backed away in lieu of Sadie's new attitude. Her confidence shattered she did her best to distance herself from me. In her mind I too

would leave and if she pushed me away and created some distance between us then it wouldn't hurt as much when I did leave. What she didn't realize was that I was madly in love with her and had no intentions of leaving her. Convincing her of this was quite a different matter.

Despite her daily tantrums and rebuffs I tried to remain positive and fulfill her needs as best I could but the winds had changed. Even our sex life changed. No longer did foreplay consist of a simple kiss and a sense of oneness when we bonded. Now and even though it was never stated our roles changed. Now foreplay consisted of her crying over the fact that no one wanted her and begging me to spank her with the belt. I'd read in some child psychology text that children abandoned their parents often blame themselves for their parents departure although this is quite often the the farthest thing from the truth. I do believe that Sadie blamed herself and was intent on being punished for chasing her mother away. And when her ass became red and swollen with welts she would turn over demanding that I fuck her.

'Harder dammit! Fuck me hard damn you! Harder!' she screamed, loud enough for the neighbors to hear.

At first I welcomed this as just another wrinkle in the many facets of my Sadie but it soon became apparent that this wasn't just a new wrinkle but the new protocol. Each time we'd make love now it began with me spanking her, each time more violently than before. Now she wanted me to enter her anally. Each time the requests demanded more and more violent encounters.

When I suggested that our love had suddenly reverted to cold, emotionless sex Sadie curled up in my arms saying that she understood completely. We agreed that every now and then she could entertain her fantasy and need for rough sex. Just not every time. And for the next month or two she seemed perfectly fine with our new agreement. Yet, despite our agreement our lovemaking became so infrequent that I called for another sit down. As soon as we sat face-to-face I realized that the best I could hope for was some semblance of the truth though in reality I knew she would only tell me what at she deemed necessary to keep me at bay.

How wrong I was.

'Is it me? Is it something I said?'

'To be perfectly honest it's not anything you at said. It's your attitude. You're such a goddamn prude. I offer you some alternatives, some variety and you turn up your nose as if you're better than I am.'

'It's not that at all.'

'If that's not it then tell me what it is?'

'I'm not sure. I just have a hard time putting my hands on a woman. I wasn't raised that way.'

'Oh please. It's not like you're doing it out of anger. I'm asking you to. It gets me hot when you spank me. Then when you hit it and beat it up that really takes me there. When you hit right I can be multi orgasmic.

'So what you're trying to tell me is that I don't satisfy if I don't beat your ass?'

She laughed reaching for the bottle of Moscato.

'Are you serious? I'm not saying that at all. I don't know what would give you that impression.'

'Well, it's been close to two months.'

'Didn't realize you were counting the days,' she said laughing again. 'Well, one thing's for sure. You don't have a clue how a woman's psyche works. We go through phases. At least I go through phases. One day I may not want to do anything but mount and ride you. That may last for a day or it could last for months until something else tickles my fancy. I'm telling you my life evolves in stages.'

'So where are we now?'

'You know where I am. I want my boyfriend to spank my ass then hit it from the back. That's I want. Now the question is can my straight laced boyfriend oblige me.'

I was stunned that she'd opened up although her explanation left a lot to be desired. And I still didn't understand her fetish with being beaten and punished.

'Baby, if that's what makes you happy then take your ass in the bedroom and lose your clothes. But before you do that answer one question for me.'

'And what is that?'

'Please tell me why it's so damn important that I beat you. Is it because you feel you've committed some grievous sin and feel like you should be punished?'

'That has to be against some type of law or another.'

'What's that?'

'The fact that you're trying to diagnose me with no medical degree. I think I'll sue you for malpractice. But seriously though, what the fuck difference does it make and why do you feel you have to make sense of everything? Why don't you stop being a little bitch. You'd think after two months without the pussy you'd be man enough to man up and take it.'

'Oh, so now we've regressed to name calling?'

'No, and I'm sorry for that but I think we need to take a break. Everything's just become so tense.   Do you realize we're basically having meetings to discuss how we are going to make love. This is just too much,' she said burying her face in her hands and crying out. 'I've got way too much on my plate right through here to be going through this shit.'

'So, that's it?'

'Yes. Baby look. You very well may be absolutely right about everything you said but in all seriousness I need a break just to gain my equilibrium.'

'Okay but you need to explain how this works since this is your brainchild.'

'No rules sweetheart. Let's just try to be civil to each other the way good roommates would do.

'Oh, so we're roommates now?'

'For now. Don't be upset with me. You know I love you. I'm just going through it now. All I'm asking for is to be patient and give me a little space. And you have to believe. If it's meant to be then it'll be. What else can I say?'

There was nothing more for her to say. She had said it all. No intrepeter was needed. If anything she'd been quite clear. I sat speechless.

'You okay baby?'

'Yeah, I'm good,' I lied. In truth I was seething. It had been quite some time since I'd been this angry. I'd relocated, changed states to be this woman, to live with this woman, to commit to this woman only to have her inform me that she no longer required my services.

'And baby...'

What more could she say that she hadn't already said. The nail was in the coffin. What was the purpose? I couldn't feel any worse.

'Listen I know you have your needs. It's only natural and I know I'm not your cup of tea right through here so if you see the need to see other people to quench your thirst I do understand and won't hold it against you.'

Suddenly I wanted to grant her wishes. I wanted to grab my belt and beat the hell out of her but I was afraid that in my present state of mind I might hurt her so I did my best to mask my emotions until I had some time to sit and think about what had just transpired.

All I knew at present was that I'd invested time, love and caring patience for over a year only to be given permission to see other women. There was no need when all I wanted was to share time with her. In a year I had received no interest or dividends on my investment. I guess I just had to chalk it up as another hurtful loss in a string of hurtful losses where women were concerned. By now you would think I would know not to put my hopes and dreams in another person. What did my mother always tell me? The only person you can depend on is yourself.

It was at this time that I came to the conclusion that I would do exactly as she requested and begin to date. What else could I do aside from sitting there pining over a woman who was unsure of the direction she wanted to take moving forward. Who was it that said never put all of your eggs in one basket and never let your heart and emotions come before your head?

I adopted this as my new philosophy moving forward. And it came at no better time as I was just starting my new job in the little town of Summerville some twenty miles outside of Charleston. In my first week of training my supervisor held a staff

meeting to introduce the new staff. There were three of us starting the other two being women. In fact, there were forty two employees. Forty of the forty two employees were

African American women, sistas all of whom were in their thirties or early forties. I considered the possibilities as I scanned the room.

I paid little or no attention to Sadie now so focused was I on righting my own ship and turning the page on that chapter of my life. The first thing I needed was a car. At present Sadie and I were sharing her cousin Bubba's old Chevy. The car wasn't much to look at but Bubba was a mechanic and the car ran like a top. I remembered Sadie telling me once that if Bubba ever knew that I was apart of her life and was driving his car that he would likely take the car. For some reason this behavior didn't seem indicative of a cousin but I never mentioned it. I needed a car.

In any case, I was to complete my training later that week and so I packed enough for the weekend and drove up early enough to do a little apartment hunting before I headed to work. I had a host of co-workers all looking trying to secure me a place of residence.

Arriving at work a few minutes later I was met by a rather tall, attractive young woman I guessed to be in her mid-twenties.

'You must be Bert. I'm Sharon,' she said thrusting out her hand. 'They said you were cute. They ain't never lied. Come on in. Let me show you around.'

I was immediately put at ease by her warm, easy nature. When she had shown me the house and told me all the do's and don'ts we retreated to the staff quarters

which was comprised of no more than a couple of wooden chairs, a desk and a bed. We sat and talked for a long time after she was off and even managed to have a sip or two from her own private cooler. She was tall and attractive standing close to six one. I eyed her and thought about the endless possibilities she handed me a slip of paper with her number on it.

'I'm in Charleston on Wednesday. Let's get together and do lunch.'

'Sounds good to me. Just call me and I'll meet you somewhere.'

'I'll do that,' she said smiling before leaning forward and kissing me on my cheek.

Driving home that weekend the future was again looking bright although Sadie's behavior was beginning to border on the bizarre even from the most liberal standpoint. Her quizzing me on my training and her need to know the names of my co-workers unnerved me.

'Sharon is the young lady that was responsible for my training.'

'How old is she?'

'I have no idea. I'd say twenty four or twenty five.'

'Oh, she's just a baby,' she said smiling and seemingly encouraged by this latest discovery. 'Do you want to fuck her?'

'Who?' I said wondering where this latest query had arisen from.

'Sharon. Don't play dumb. You know exactly who I'm referring to.'

'I hadn't considered it. You know I don't make it a habit to work and play in the same place.'

Oh, please. You're a man and men are dogs. She gives you a hint that you can have it and you're on it. There ain't no rules when it comes to y'all getting your dick licked,' she stated rather matter-of-factly.

I did not respond.

'So, are you going to fuck her?'

'I don't know Sadie. I never gave it any thought,' I said annoyed at her persistence. It had been close to three months since we'd slept together and sex was the last thing I wanted to talk about especially with her.

'Okay. You don't have to answer. There are something's a woman just knows. Call it women's intuition. Call it whatever you like but I know that it's just a matter of time. When you do sleep with her just let me know if the pussy's as good as this.' she said easing down on top of me and taking all of me into her warm, throbbing chasm.

I was sitting in the living room in front of the bay window when she mounted me. After taking her blouse and bra off she opened the drapes for the world to see. This was her new passion. On more than one occasion I'd arrive at home to find her breasts mashed up against the bay window while she masturbated with cucumbers, wine bottles, hair brushes or anything at hand.

I wasn't so much worried about her as I'd found an apartment and would be moving within the next week but I knew she had nowhere to go should someone catch her and report her. I'm not sure whether she took heed or not but I made it no secret that I was leaving.

I was packing when the phone rang.

'I know you didn't think I was going to call you.'

'Hey Sharon. Nice to hear from.'

'You busy?'

'Not really. Just packing.'

'So, you're really serious about moving to Summerville?'

'I am.'

'Okay. You're going to be bored out of your mind. Don't say I didn't warn you you. But anyway I'm just calling to see if you wanted to do lunch?'

'Absolutely. I need a break from packing anyway.'

'And to think I thought you might be glad just to see me.'

'I can't wait,' I laughed. 'Give me an address.'

Twenty minutes later I was downtown searching for the restaurant. I knew downtown fairly well but for the life of me I couldn't place a restaurant at the address she'd given me. There was a reason for that. There was no restaurant at that address. In

it's place stood a rundown motel. I smiled at Sharon's cleverness which had lured me downtown only to realize that I was to be lunch.

Moments later I entered the room on the third floor and was pleasantly surprised to see Sharon looking even better than when I'd last seen her. Her hair and makeup were done. Aside from that she wore nothing. Beckoning me to the bed she said nothing. Her smile said it all as she reached for me and took me inside of her. I gasped doing my best to catch my breath in between rounds and still no words had passed between us.

We spent the better part of the afternoon exploring each other's needs and desires until we were totally and unequivocally satisfied.

'I knew from the minute we met that it was going to be good but that was delicious. Anytime you want a do over or to revisit my treasure chest again you be sure to pick up the phone and call me.'

'You didn't do too bad yourself Ms. Locklear,' I said squeezing her tightly.

Her words had done my ego a world of good especially when I was beginning to doubt the worth of my own manhood.

Arriving home that evening I was still glowing and call it a woman's intuition but the first thing out of Sadie's mouth was, 'You fucked her didn't you?'

My second thought was why would she ask me? Wasn't it she that set the rule that there were no rules. Hadn't she given me permission to be with other women. And

if that woman were her would she appreciate me telling a third party that we had just had sex. So, why the third degree?

I couldn't respond. I wasn't ignoring her or trying to be rude. It was simply so uncanny that she would surmise our having sex and after much badgering I admitted that I had.

'Was it good?'

I was purposely ignoring her now.

'Did she scream? Did you make her scream your name? Did she tell you she loved you? Just tell me if she screamed.'

I didn't know if this was just another wrinkle in her sordid fantasies but their was little doubt that she was more aroused than angry. The more she clamored for details the more intent I was on keeping her at bay until I had had enough.

'If I'd known you were this interested I would have taken you with me so you could watch.

Picking up on my sarcasm she smiled devilishly.

'No. There's no need for me to tag along. Just show me how you fucked her,' she said sliding the pants to her two piece lounge outfit to the floor before bending over the dining room table. I moved up behind and eased my hard shaft into her warm, pulsating vagina.

'No baby. I want it in the other hole. Put it in my ass.'

There was no love in this but she seemed happy as she screamed 'harder' with each stroke. I did as I was told somehow knowing that would be the last time as I felt nothing. Crying for me to spank her I could not commit to this at which time she began cursing me.

'You punk ass bitch,' she said slapping me hard against my face. The burning sting from the slap angered me but I refused to respond. This is what she really wanted. Me to grow so anger that without thinking I'd grab her and beat her ass.

Still, I refused to lift a hand even after she slapped me several more times in an attempt to get a rise out of me. Instead I pulled out headed for the shower and decided to call it a night.

Sadie had other plans and stood outside of the bathroom door shouting obscenities and listing all of my shortcomings and inadequacies.

The following Monday was the first of the month. I had already secured an apartment and was in the process of moving in. I knew that it was time as Sadie's behavior became more and more bizarre with her now apologizing and asking me if I still loved her.

I'd previously concluded that as much as I loved her there was no denying that Sadie had some deep-seated emotional problems that I was in noway equipped to deal with. I hardly spoke to her at all now and was antsy about moving. Still, the quieter I got the more Sadie talked. If anyone watching didn't know they would swear we were the perfect couple.

It was always this way, with the apologies first before she'd fall to her knees in hopes of pleasing me and erasing all the mean and hurtful things she hurled at me during her tirade. I have never openly responded believing in the good Lord and the Law of Kharma to remedy the meanness hurled at me. I, however, have never wished any ill will towards Sadie. After all despite her troubles I still loved her so I did as I always did and let it pass.

The next morning I awoke to a cheerful Sadie fixing breakfast.

'I'm running late sweetie. Your breakfast is in the microwave,' she said kissing me before heading out the door. 'Oh, and by the way, don't work too hard. I'm gonna need you to have all your energy tonight. I've got something very special planned for you,' she said winking at me and grinning sheepishly.

'Have a good one,' I said hoping to hasten her exit.

It was the same every time. It began with the screaming and yelling and her having a temper tantrum if things didn't proceed the way she wanted them to in the bedroom. The apology would follow and then the next day she would open up with a heartfelt soul expose explaining her behavior but by this time there was no explanation needed. By this time I had fostered a prognosis. It was simple but accurate. The bitch was crazy. I knew the routine.

Tonight she would come in smiling and be all lovey dovey before going to take a shower and coming out in a policeman's uniform complete with handcuffs. Or maybe tonight she'd be a nurse. By now this had become all too common and a bit too eccentric for my blood. I was a simple guy and all I needed to know was that she loved me. That was enough foreplay for me. There was no need to dress up or role play. I love you just the way you are. To comment concerning this latest bit of deviancy could result in World War III so I had gone along with it more often than not but by this time I had grown weary and wondered why we just couldn't play us when it came to lovemaking. It didn't matter now though. I had one foot out the door.

Climbing the two flights of stairs that evening to the apartment I turned the key not knowing what to expect. I just prayed that she didn't have anything on the agenda. I was exhausted. What I found instead was our normally pristine little chapel in shambles.

'Sadie.' I yelled hoping that she had survived. I found her sitting on the edge of the tub holding an ice bag to her right eye.

'Sweetie are you alright?'

She nodded that she was and I was immediately relieved.

'What happened?'

'Bubba.'

'Your cousin Bubba?' I asked puzzled now.

'Yes. He called and said he wanted to stop by and check on the car and make sure everything was okay. When I invited him in to get the key he started asking me about you and well one thing led to another as you can see,' she said removing the ice pack from her eye.

'But what caused it?'

'He said I used him for his car. He said that he gave me the car and that when I got settled in I was supposed to give him a call. It was all news to me but he said I'd agreed to that.'

'Well let's just be glad that's all the damage he did.'

Sadie broke out in tears and thundering sobs that made me wish I hadn't said anything.

'Stop! Baby stop. It's all over baby,' I repeated over and over to no avail.

'You don't understand Bert. He raped me. I know you don't care but what man wants a rape victim. I'll tell you. No man wants a woman who's been raped,' she said between shuddering sobs that made her shoulders heave.

'Sadie. Sadie. Sadie. What he did was wrong and he will be judged and prosecuted for his actions. But you did nothing wrong so don't go blaming yourself.'

'Would you have sex with someone knowing that they had been raped? It's almost as if it's cursed, almost as if it's been tainted.'

'And again that's not the woman's fault.'

'Then answer me.'

'Yes I would if I loved her.'

'Do you love me?'

'You already know the answer to that.' I knew where she was going with this and sought to quell her latest attempts at reconciliation. It was too late for that and her once sexy body now repelled me with all my passion having dissipated towards her. 'If you love me then let me hear you say it. If any day I need to hear it it's today.'

'You know I love you Sadie.'

'Then why are you leaving me?' She said the tears beginning to flow again.

'Can I tell you a story sweetheart?'

'Make it quick.'

'I had a friend back in the day His name was Gary. We called him 'G'. Now Gary and I were thick as thieves and stayed in some shit. I'd go to jail one week. He'd go the next. True story. We were headed the wrong way and we were leading each other down the path to destruction. Anyway, one day his dad pulled our coats. He said it's obvious that you two love each other but if you really love each other you'll go your separate ways because if you stay together you're going to be the death of each other. And you know he was right.'

'And you told me that story why?'

'Because I realize that as much as I love you that if I continue down this path you will likely be the death of me.'

'Oh, Bert,' she laughed. 'You're so dramatic.'

'I'm dead serious.'

'Oh come on. Am I really that bad?'

'Not saying that bay. I just think we're on two different conflicting paths. I've wrestled with and come to terms with both my God and my demons. He has blessed me and shown me inner peace. It is up to me to maintain that peace.'

'And you can't do that with me?'

'I tried. I tried to both love and understand you. But anytime I seemed to get close you pushed me away. I watched as her shoulders heaved up and down and knew she was crying again.'

'Now I wish I hadn't said anything especially after the kind of day you had.

Sadie dropped her head and though there was no sound I watched as her shoulders heaved up and down and knew that she was crying again.

'The day I had. The day I had. I was beaten and raped. My house was trashed during the whole affair and my man wants to leave me because I'm a mess. And you make it sound like it was just any other day.'

'I'm sorry. I didn't mean to sound so cold and unfeeling.'

'You can't help it. That's just who you are. But try to wrap your little mind around this. I was beaten, then made to have sex against my will. In other words I was raped you cold, unfeeling bastard!' She said now screaming at the top of her lungs.

I dropped my head. I knew she was hurt but there was nothing I could do other than sit and lend an ear. We sat in silence for close to an hour with me holding her and attempting to console her.

'Is there anything I can do sweetheart?'

'Actually there is. Pour me a glass of wine and take off your clothes for me . And don't say a word.'

I did as directed and prayed this would be the the last time. Pouring her a glass of Moscato I heard the shower. By the time she got out of the shower I was half way though my second bottle of wine. I didn't know what I expected to emerge from the shower but I was lit and it didn't much matter. To my surprise there was no costume but the simple black two piece teddy outfit I liked so much. I could feel myself harden at the sight of her. Wasting little time she let her lingerie bottoms drop to the floor exposing her pretty, round chocolate ass. Reaching me she grabbed my hardened eased down engulfing all of me. I responded in kind meeting her every thrust with one of my own. She was teasing now allowing only the tip to enter and each time I would try to penetrate her deeply she would pull away. As you can probably surmise I was beside myself by this time.

'Baby please,' I was demeaned to begging now but the demonic forces in her must have charged me with something, perhaps for leaving her, but I was being punished and made to pay.

Begging and pleading helped little so once again I was made to bend my will to her desires. Sadie must have known this was the last time and seemed to determine to take full advantage of that fact while driving me crazy in the interim. She was quite successful riding the tip and stopping at regular intervals when I began to moan loudly or she deemed me on the verge of climaxing. This went on for what seemed like forever and I was literally on the verge of tears when she stopped.

'So, Mr. Brown I hear you want to leave this sweet pussy. Is that true?'

Before I could answer she started her methodic attempts at driving me insane. She was in control. She knew it and had no intention of letting me off the hook until I'd given up this foolish notion of leaving her or so she thought. And then as if she'd been sent a signal she took all of me, slamming herself down on my swollen and throbbing shaft. By the time she eased down on me for the third time I was gushing like a fountain. I don't remember much of anything after that but I am quite certain I passed out. I remember her smiling at me after I'd come and was spent.

'What my man feels to realize is that Sadie May is multi-talented and will have whatever she sets her sights on. Remember that. I'm not finished with you yet Mr. Brown'. And after what she'd just done to me I was inclined to agree.

Well that is up until the grand opening of Charleston's new Black Cultural Arts Center downtown. It was a black tie affair so that Sunday Sadie and I put on our best clothes and headed downtown. I was content to stand on the balcony sipping a glass of

Merlot and watch the lobby fill with the Black elite. You could actually see the money as women sashayed to and fro in their thousand dollar gowns. But there was one particular woman who caught my attention and stood out from the rest. She had to be in her early seventies with caramel, pecan skin. Donning a light blue tunic with gold embroidery an d a matching head wrap she epitomized a simple elegance. To me she epitomized what African royalty must have looked like. To me she had the regal-Ness of an African queen much in the same way Lena Horne and Cicely Tyson do.

I called Sadie to see and share my experience.

'Look!' I said pointing to the stately, older woman sure Sadie would share in my glee. It was my first time being in a room with so many wealthy, well-to-do Black folks.

'Look at the woman in the light blue gown. She's sharp as a tack.' I said pointing to the woman. Sadie's response was not what I was expecting.

'You want to fuck her don't you?' she screamed. Everyone's head turned in my direction. I must admit I have never been so embarrassed in all my life. 'Go ahead and fuck her then. I always knew you were nothing but a little whore. Go ahead and fuck her. You have my permission.'

I was numb, in a state of shock and found that I was glued to my spot overlooking the lobby. I couldn't move. I wanted to run away from the hundreds of eyes that were condemning me on what this lunatic spouted to the world. I wanted to run and found that I could not. My legs were frozen, unable to move and carry me away from Sadie's profanity filled tirade.

'Why don't you suck her pussy too. You're good at that you bitch ass motherfucker.'

The only thing that seemed to quiet her down were the two burly Black policemen who each grabbed an arm and led her away.

One brother who witnessed the entire event walked up to me and patted me on the back.

'Don't feel bad. Alot of brothers wouldn't have waited for the police. They would have beaten her ass for disrespecting them in public.'

It didn't make me feel any better as I made my way to the car. I waited forty-five minutes and when Sadie didn't appear I headed home only to find her already there.

'I'm sorry sweetie,' she said doing her best to corner and kiss me.

'No Sadie. Not tonight. I know you may have a hard time believing this but sex is not the answer to everything.'

'Oh come on sweetheart. There's nothing better than make-up sex,' she said untying her robe and exposing her more than ample breasts as she moved closer.

'No baby. All the make-up sex in the world can't make up for the embarrassment you caused me tonight.'

'Let Sadie May try daddy. I know I fucked up but just give me the chance to make it better. Let Sadie make you forget. Just let me love you bay.'

'No Sadie. This was the straw that broke the camels back.'

'So, in other words we're done?'

'After tonight's performance I wouldn't even think that you'd have to ask.'

'So, you're really going leave me?'

'Just as soon as I can.'

I wasn't angry. Just tired. Oh, so tired. And I saw nothing to suggest that she was getting any better. That night I listened to Sadie's pleading as she banged on my bedroom door.

'Baby please don't leave me. I'll get help. I promise I'll get help. Just have a little more patience with me. Baby I promise I'll make you happy again. It'll be like it used to be in the beginning. Are you listening? I know I have problems bay. But I'm going to get help tomorrow. I'm not going to put it off another day. I need to go now. Baby just tell me what to do. I'll do whatever you like bay but please don't leave me.'

When I didn't respond she went into another tirade repeating all the foul perversities she'd recited earlier that evening.

'You're not leaving me because of how I acted tonight. You're leaving because you don't know a goddamn thing about love. That lil no good ho gave you some and you don't know if you're in love or just a goddamn playa at this point. But what you are is a dog. A motherfuckin' bitch ass dog. But that's okay you go ahead and fuck Sharon and anyone else you want. I don't care anymore,' Sadie cried walking into her own bedroom.

The following day was Monday, the first. I waited until Sadie was on her way to work to move my last load to my new apartment.

It's been close to nine months since I last talked to Sadie. Seems her mother relocated to Atlanta. Sadie later moved and now resides in Atlanta.

Tommy's a Girl

The last we spoke I was moving to Summerville. I've been here a good six months and I absolutely love it. I reside on Main Street in an adults only apartment complex. Across the street is an up scale crab shack that I considered my home away from home. It was the kind of place you took a first date for a warm, relaxed but lively environment.

Now I don't know if I mentioned the fact that I was one of two males on a staff of forty two with the remaining forty being Black women. Most if not all were friendly single, and approachable.

I loved my apartment and its proximity to the crab shack across the street. I loved the fact that my new co-workers warmly and gracious welcomed me. A few even managed to stop by unexpectedly and unannounced.

My phone rang constantly and I never lacked for something to do. Alicia a pretty, dark-skinned, country girl introduced herself and became a regular stopping by almost every day although it was difficult for me to get a fix on where she was coming from and still I allowed her to stay in my company. I was leery of most women by this time. Either they appeared to be 'normal' and had skeletons their closet or they had

ulterior motives that drove them. Black men were at a premium. And a Black man with not one but two jobs, good credit and no record was a rarity. I didn't necessary think I was anything special but I did possess all of the qualities I mentioned heretofore.

So, and even though she stopped by daily I still had my reservations about Alicia. And one of my reservations was her age. Alicia was twenty two and I was thirty four. I hadn't taught in years and I had no desire to go back to teaching and especially a young woman who someone had informed was cute. That may have been the problem. All her laurels rested on the thought that she was God's gift to the rest of us and this may have been her biggest flaw. She was arrogant in her ignorance.

Her best friend, an older girl about my age talked frankly to me about Alicia warning me.

'I was wondering how long it would take her to gravitate your way.'

'Excuse me.'

'I was wondering how long it would take before Alicia made eyes for you. It's no secret she likes older guys with a little something in their pocket so she can live like the diva she thinks she is. All I'm telling you is to be careful. Some women can be treacherous but then I'm sure you can handle your own.'

'Thanks for the heads up.'

'No problem and like I said be careful.'

I have never understood why this woman who proclaimed to be Alicia's best friend would see fit to warn me about her. Still, I didn't take this advice lightly especially from someone who had known her all of her life. And for this reason we never grew really close. I could never let my guard down and be myself for fear of some chink in my armor being exposed leaving me susceptible. She, on the other had little or nothing to lose whether she was sincere in her forays into talk of relationships and marriage I have no idea but I steered clear of those conversations and kept her at bay for the most part.

We slept together regularly but it was no more than that. Two adults that shared the warmth of each other's bodies and the long conversations that put an end to boredom and loneliness. Still, the more time we spent together the more she began talking of taking the next step.

'I'm twenty-three and I think I've sowed all the wild oats the good Lord put here for me. And I know this may sound crazy to you coming from someone my age but I'm tired. I'm tired of running these streets and going from one crazy relationship to the next. I'm tired of the club scene and the games. Like I said I'm just tired.'

'There's no reason you can't take a break and put everything on hold for a minute.'

'I already have. I did that when I decided to become your woman.'

'Is that right?' I said preferring to defer from this conversation.

'You know it is. My life consists of me going to work and when I'm off I'm here with you.'

'I was beginning to notice that.'

'And you know what's funny about that?'

'No what's funny about that?'

'A couple of years ago I knew this guy who wanted me to do exactly that. he wanted me to move in and basically be a kept woman. At the time I thought that was so lame but I don't know now. You never asked me to move in but if you were to I think I would like that. I don't know what it is but I really enjoy your company and if you ever decided to let your guard down and let me in I would like to think that we could carve out a rather nice life for us. You may even decide that you want to marry me and have kids. I think that would be nice.'

'Goodness. Where did all of that come from?'

'My heart and soul baby. Let's take this to the next stage. Trust me. This little girl can keep up. I will make you happy Bert.'

What she didn't realize was that after six years with Chris' mom and another year and a half with Sadie I was pretty sure that relationship just weren't for me. Still, Alicia pressed on.

During the time I was seeing Alicia the company employed another young Black man named Lloyd who wove his way into our inner circle. Lloyd lived a fair

distance from the job he would stay over and on more than one occasion so as not to have to make the hour drive that night only to have to turn around and come back the following morning.

I can remember one time Lloyd decided to stay over. Alicia and I were already there and chances were better than average that if she and I were there then we were in bed. That's where we were when Lloyd arrived. So, he laid down at the foot of the bed and joined us watching television. Now aside from her coming over and jumping in bed I had no idea why Alicia saw fit to visit daily. I couldn't figure her out although one thing was quite apparent. Alicia didn't like Lloyd. She looked at him as an intrusion into her world.

Annoyed that Lloyd was there Alicia fell asleep before the movie was over. Several hours later I was awakened by Alicia's soft pliable hands and mouth fondling and kissing every inch of me. No longer able to feign sleep I took her into my arms and made heated love to her which shook the bed and made her scream at regular intervals before we passed out, sex funky, and drenched in sweat. If there was one place we were compatible it was in bed.

Outside of bed she was a hellion with the mouth of a sailor. She was usually angry with something or another and lately her wrath had been directed at me. But I ignored her for the most part. She fulfilled a need in me so I put everything else on hold where she was concerned. She had to be one of the most attractive women I've ever had the chance to be around. She was also one of the angriest I'd ever have the occasion to know. And when she couldn't lure me into her web of marriage I became the object of

her anger.

What I couldn't understand was why she kept coming around if I annoyed her so. What puzzled me was why I couldn't just walk away from her. Was it my fear of being alone? Was it my fear of losing my sexual partner? Did I subconsciously enjoy the daily battles, arguments and drama that she brought with her? Or was it her youth and vitality? I'm not sure if it were any one of these or a culmination of all of these? I didn't know. Here's how a typical day would unfold.

She would usually call early in the morning but instead of a rather chipper 'hello' or 'good morning' she would call and curse me out for something or another she'd let fester for days or weeks. When she'd finish addressing whatever angered her she' d hang up on me. I hated having anyone angry at me for anything so I'd call her back and tell her to come and see me so we could come to some agreement and some sense of peace.

Forty five minutes later she would knock, before entering and quickly disrobe. I assumed from this that whatever had been on her mind was now resolved. She would do everything possible to make me the happiest man in the world, well, at least for the night.

I was fine with this although I never did understand with all her blessed good looks why she was so unhappy. I couldn't help her. She never talked or opened up to let me know what was going on with her. And if she did open up it was always around something negative. Lloyd noticed this too and made a point to tell me that the only thing he'd ever heard say anything positive was when he was trapped at the bottom of the bed and she was screaming, 'Yes daddy. Right there daddy. That's the spot.'

'But seriously Bert. You be careful with that girl. Alicia has a negative spirit and believe me you don 't want that to enter you or your home. Seriously though, she has an evil karma about her that you should really avoid. It's not healthy. I can' exactly pinpoint what it is but I'd steer clear of her just to be on the safe side. There are plenty of other women out there. You know Tommy's feeling you but Alicia 'no'.

Lloyd was my boy. I knew he both loved and cared about me. We'd grown tight over the past few months so I knew it had nothing to do with jealousy or anything of that nature. No. He saw the same things that I did though we couldn't pinpoint exactly what the problem was that was making everyone uncomfortable we were acutely aware that there was something troubling Alicia.

'Seriously though B you know as well as I do that that girl is evil.'

'I hear you,' was the best I could muster.

I was the one around her the most and would have had to have been deaf, dumb and blind not to have noticed by now. She was hard, ghetto and scandalous opting to seduce an unknowing victim with her seductive attractiveness and sex.

I was aware of all this so what Lloyd and others were beginning to point out were mere redundancies. In my case, the question which still went unanswered was what she wanted from me. I worked two full time jobs just to make ends meet like most of he people I knew. And I knew this would hardly be enough to maintain the style of life she demanded. I certainly couldn't help maintain her lifestyle. Seems she was adamant about her financial security and being wealthy by any means necessary. I thought this to be somewhat far-fetched with her having a high school diploma, still living at home and spending her entire salary on clothes and accessories to flaunt back home. Perhaps someone would fall victim to her seductive charm and fulfill all her needs. That person, however, would not be me. And yet I refused to let go almost as if there some secret bond or need that kept me in contact.

'Bert baby why don't you come up and see me and how my peeps are living. Seriously why don't you come visit me. If I'm not working I'm usually somewhere along the wall. That's where everyone goes on the weekend.'

I knew it was all just talk but I was curious as to her mercurial changes in mood and so I decided to drive up hoping to get some insight into this woman I allowed to share

my bed. I recruited Lloyd who wasn't doing anything and he agreed to take the half an hour drive up to surprise Alicia. Her girlfriend gave us directions.

'Don't go up there Bert. There's nothing there but trouble. Just a bunch of ghetto niggas drinkin' and gettin' high then shootin' and stabbin' each other. I'm telling you it's not the place you want to be.'

'If for any reason it doesn't look kosher I'm out. Trust me I'm not lookin' for any trouble.'

'Then don't go.'

'Have a good night Keneisha.'

'You be careful Bert. I'm tellin' you those niggas are crazy.'

For the past week or two Alicia and I had been playing phone tag. I chose to listen to the voicemails rather than to actively engage her nonsense.

There was one person I did answer the phone for however. Her name was Sivitra. A graduate of Charleston Southern, she was an attractive woman with an infectious smile and she was my best friend. She too worked for Dorchester County Mental Retardation but she was not part of the inner circle although she was fairly well-known and respected by all but she played no games and tended to be aloof and distant. Well, at least that how she appeared to everyone else. What I saw and believe me she would never agree but I just thought that she knew she brought more to the table than most and simply refused to lower herself to their level. Whatever it was we found enjoyment in each other's company. What I liked most about her was that she could think and put life in perspective. We talked of each other's mates and I learned so much from her, from a woman's perspective.

'Help me to understand things from a male's perspective,' and being as straightforward and honest as I could be I would tell her if her so-called boyfriend was using her and playing games or if he was as sincere as he professed to be. Sivitra would listen to me reaffirm what she already knew but it hardly mattered. She was in love. She was a bright, astute young lady and she could easily see as many holes in my relationship as I could see in hers with one slight difference. I was not in a relationship. My heart was not involved with any of the women I was sleeping with.

Sivitra understood but still criticized me for being around the likes of Alicia and Sharon.

'Tell me something. In Alicia's case please tell me aside from her looks what's the attraction?'

'I wish I knew.'

'That's a damn shame. You know I don't blame her. She's reaching, trying to climb out of her life and ascend. She sees you as her ticket out but you have little or no use for her dumb ass aside from sex and she's so young and dumb that she can't even see what's happening.' As far as you're concerned don't you think you're selling yourself short Bert? You deserve so much better.' 'I agree but the person that I share my innermost thoughts with seems to be taken.'

'Is that right? Perhaps you didn't make it clear to her what you expected from her.

'If that's the case then let me see if I can make it clear.' I said grabbing her and pulling her into the staff bedroom. '

'Oh, my, Mr. Brown. What are you doing?'

'I'm trying to get to know my best friend from another perspective.'

Sitting her on the edge of the bed I kissed Sivitra while I unbuttoned her blouse.

'Oh, Mr. Brown,' she said gasping as I took her breast in my mouth.

'I just hope I can satisfy you. I aim to please.'

'Well, let me help you,' Sivitra whispered just loud enough for me to hear as she stood up and eased her panties down to her ankles before stepping out of them and hiking her skirt up to reveal her freshly shaved, caramel, pussy. I immediately unbuckled my belt and let my pants fall and pulled her to the edge of the bed.

Entering her slowly and deliberately I found her to be more than just a little receptive.

'Ooh, Mr. Brown,' she giggled. 'That is good. No wonder Alicia keeps coming back.'

I smiled and watched as her eyes closed and the smile spread across her face. An occasional scream on her part was all I needed to let me know she was ecstatic. Still, I had to cover her mouth so as not to wake the clients. I had never experienced anyone

quite like Sivitra. To say she was vocal was an understatement. It was certainly a boon to my ego. But after trying to muffle her cries with a pillow she was still loud and even her muffled screams were loud enough to wake my clients. I must admit that I was even happier than she was in the way that she'd responded on our first encounter but despite her calm reserved appearance on the job she was anything but discreet tonight.

After calming both Sivitra and my clients making sure that they were in bed I returned to the staff quarters where I found Sivitra sitting up. Entering she lay back down and proceeded to lift her skirt back up. I knelt down between her legs and began kissing her inner thighs. Moaning softly now she opened her eyes.

'Oh, Bert I didn't know. You do that too? You are full of surprises aren't you? If you were worried about me waking your clients before you might want to save this for a later date. You kiss me there and I swear I'll let the entire neighborhood know. In case you haven't guessed it's been close to a year since I'v had any love and never have I had someone love me the way you have. I could get hooked very easily. Allyou would have to do is say you want me. I'm sure we could work it out where you could have me on lock down should you you choose to have me.'

'Sounds almost too good to be true. But I want it to be right and with J.C. and Billy running around it's not really conducive to me loving you the way you should be loved.

Truth is Sivitra was close to eleven years younger than I was although I was unaware of this at the time. She was truly a novice when it came to matters of the flesh but was a ready and willing participant. Still, it was quite apparent she was disappointed in this latest development.

'So, what you're saying is you're sending me home with my hormones on fire and me wanting you more now than at anytime since we met.'

'So, you mean this is not the first time you've thought about the two of us and yet you never thought to mention it.'

'No. To be honest I've thought about it on the regular but every time I get up the nerve to bring it up you're involved with someone new.'

'And not one of them holds a candle to you.'

'So, why didn't you think to approach me?'

'I have on more than one occasion but I didn't want to risk our friendship.'

'Fair enough but I'm pretty sure you're still not feeling that way so where do we go from here?'

I stood up and went to my wallet and took my spare house key out and placed it in her hand.

'What's this for?'

'This is the key to my apartment. Take it. Go home and get clothes for work this week. You're spending the week with me and we'll talk about where we go from here when I get home and I have some other unfinished business to tend to.'

'Oh. I can hardly wait but let me ask you this. Who else has a key to your apartment?'

'Just you. I don't give my key out.'

'You gave it to me.'

'You're not just anyone.'

'And I'm going show you that when you get home,' she said smiling and kissing me on the cheek.

'I can't wait.'

I walked her to to the door and began the countdown.

I loved Sivitra but she always seemed to be just out of reach. She was in love with some guy. I think he was in the navy but whoever he was he had her nose wide open. We talked almost daily and although she had relinquished her heart to him he was unfeeling and took her for granted. She knew this and was seemingly at the end of the road when she gave herself to me. I was still enjoying my new found freedom and she was talking of a relationship.

I hadn't heard from Alicia in weeks and it was just as well. Lloyd and I had driven up to the hole-in-the wall and found her draped over some guy and that was all I needed to see. I never mentioned anything about it although I'm sure Lloyd let everyone know that I'd caught Alicia red handed with another man.

I guess, (and I say this with no ego or arrogance), that the escapades of my follies was the stuff that tabloids and gossip lived on. Even my supervisor was curious.

'Bert I'm just curious about something. If it's too personal just say so and I'll leave it alone but are you still seeing Sharon? She's a very nice young woman and one of my hardest workers. She's had a hard time and I'd just like to see her happy. You know you could do a lot worse.'

'I'll keep that in mind,' was the best I could do.

Sivitra was a different story. Because she kept to herself little was known about her other than the fact that she was a college student who lived alone in Charleston. Her business was her own. As aloof and distant as she appeared we had somehow found each other and hadn't been afraid to open up and share our most inner most fears and secrets. In a short time we had become the closest of friends enjoying each other's minds and

warm, open conversations. We were more like siblings than friends. Well, it had been more like siblings until last night.

What I liked most about her was that she was an old soul whose parents divorced early in her life. This was only one of many of many hurts and disappointments in Sivitra's life. In fact, Sivitra had grown so used to the hurt that she'd

compartmentalized the pain dismissing it more often than not as just another of life's twists.

I'd known her for about seven or eight months. We spoke almost daily and she would stop by regularly to sit and talk and not once had I had the occasion to entertain her as anything other than a dear friend.

Now I could hardly contain my excitement. I was thrilled that she would be home waiting for me when I got home. We'd always been comfortable in each other's company but for some reason I was more than a little nervous about going home to my house, to my best friend. I knew in large part my nervousness was due to the script being written beforehand. That is I knew that I was going home and that Sivitra would be there waiting and expecting me to take her to sexual paradise. I guess what I objected to most were the expectations I'd placed on myself.

The truth of the matter is there was no emotional link between Sivitra and myself. She didn't love me and the truth of the matter is I didn't love her or better yet I wasn't in love with her and now I was questioning why I had initiated anything. I'm sure it was no more than curiosity on her part but I had long since given up having sex for the sake of having sex. The days of challenging myself to see if I was capable were long gone. There was no longer that need for conquest and I certainly wasn't interested in a relationship so what was this? If there wasn't something; a bond, a union of love, a need to be with that person out of passion and a belief that this person was your soul mate then

I saw no reason to bear my soul and the most intimate part of my being with them.

I truly believed this although I hadn't always but it was essential to who I was

now. And so I questioned the reason I was going home to Sivitra.

Turning the key I entered my sparse but tastefully decorated apartment. It really

felt good to have someplace to be able to call home. It didn't hurt to have a

beautiful woman waiting either although after considerable thought I was adamant

about diffusing the impending situation.

'Sivitra.'

'In the bedroom and could you please grab the bottle of wine and a glass. There

were two full bottles of wine in the fridge. She must have bought them I surmised

before joining her in the bedroom.

She sat on the edge of my bed in a pair of heels and my robe.

'Damn baby you look even better than when I left you last night. Is that possible?'

she said grinning broadly. 'Come here lover,' she said beckoning me to come

closer.

I kissed her and pulled away as soon as slid down in the bed.

'If I remember correctly you promised me something Mr. Brown.'

'And what could that be?'

'Don't play dumb Mr. Brown. I want you to finish what you started last night.'

'Oh that,' I said laughing nervously and trying to buy some time. "I'll see what I can do but let me grab a quick shower,' I said stepping into the bathroom and turning on the shower.

'No need for that sweetie. That'll just be a waste 'cause when I get finished with you you're really going to need one. What did Jill Scott call it in her book? Yeah, we gonna get sex funky.'

'Is that right?' I said stepping into the shower.

Drying off and stepping back into the bedroom I found Sivitra half dressed. My surprise must have shown.

'What? It's clear you don't want me Mr. Brown so I guess I'll take my starvin' ass

home,' she said dropping her head. I couldn't see her face but I was sure she was

crying now. 'Wow. I really played myself didn't I?'

'No, not at all. But what gave you the impression that I don't want you?'

'Oh come on Bert. Who knows you better than I do and I know that you don't

want me. You made that quite obvious last night when you chased me away from

the group home and gave me your key so I wouldn't feel bad. To make matters

worse I haven't had an orgasm in more than a year and you stop right when I was

on the verge of one. I've been laying here throbbing and waiting for you to come

home since I left you. And then you come home and act like I'm not here. What

am I supposed to think?

You were probably hoping I wasn't here when you got home but you're going to

acknowledge me and not just brush me off the way you do the rest of those chicken

heads in your fan club.'

'Why are you trippin' Sivitra?' I said smiling. She was bright and perceptive as

hell. Any man that wold take her on would certainly have his hands full. She'd make you do more than think. Sivitra would have a brotha doing mental gymnastics.

'You woke up my boys and you know how Billy and T.J. are. The first thing they want to do is run to Janet and say Bert had women in the house the other night. The way you were yelling they could have probably heard you in Myrtle Beach and that was with a mouth full of pillow.'

I could see her smiling now.

'Well, damn it was good and like I said it's been awhile. But okay I'll give you a pass on that one but explain how a man comes home and walks past a beautiful, young woman lying naked in his bed. Seriously. Who does that?'

'Stop that,' I shouted knowing she was right and I was guilty. 'You know I've been following you around like an orphaned puppy for close to a year and anytime I tried to make a move you threw Jake up in my face.'

'It's James.'

'Jake, James, whatever.'

'You're right. I did hat because I was attracted to you and was trying to stay faithful. Besides you had too many of your fan club and groupies hanging around for me to get caught up in the mix. I don't share. But now that you've taken a sabbatical I'm curious to see if there's any grounds for the hype.'

'So, that's what this is all about.'

'I'm teasing. Goodness. I'm teasing you sweetie. Why are you so tense? Have a sip of wine and come hold me.'

I was feeling some kind of way about what she said and didn't think it a joke and wondered how much was how she really felt when she said she was curious as to all the hype surrounding the new kid on the block. Sure I recognized that I was the new kid on the block who everyone wanted to play with. And when the word got out that I was a descent Black guy who had his own and could handle himself in and out of the bedroom they came out of the woodwork. Now here was my confidante and friend that I confided in and shared my love life or lack thereof telling me she was curious as well. I felt somehow betrayed. To think she was having those very same thoughts after me having told her how I'd gone from being a person when I first arrived to an object that was good in bed. This was never more evident than the time I'd gotten out of bed with one of my dear friends whose name shall remain private. In any case, we had just had sex and I was heading to take a shower when I remembered I didn't have my shaving gear and stepped back into the bedroom. She was already on the phone.

'Girl he's good. I'm telling you he got skills. Broke the bone out my back,' she said not even trying to conceal the fact that our privacy had just become community news.

Now Sivitra was objectifying me but it was more than that with her. She was adamant about receiving some sex. She was horny beyond belief and what could it hurt. He was the closest person to her and her best friend. She loved him but was not in love with him although there was little doubt in her mind that the only base left uncovered was the question of their compatibility in the bedroom and now that he had initiated it she was certainly going to find out if all the talk was true. If it was she would learn to love him.

She, after all, had an advantage over all the rest. She was in his inner sanctum of one. She held a special place in his heart and soul. She after all was his best friend and was the shoulder he cried on, his sounding board but most of all she was his friend and although she had said nothing in the past of her feelings towards him she had come to realize she was in love with him if he was not in love with her.

Still, that was a temporary situation that she would and could correct. She would be so good to him that he would have no choice but to fall in love with her. And now that he'd sown his oats she would wrap him up in a swaddling blanket of her love and take him the rest of the journey until death do they part.

'Come here sweetie?' Sivitra said beckoning to me.

I was confused but she wasn't.

'Are you going to make love to your girl?'

'If that's what my girl wants,' I heard myself say.'

'Before you do that would you finish what you started last night.'

'What's that?' I asked knowing full well what she wanted.

'You know when you started kissing my inner thighs. I really like that.'

'Relax honey and let's just see where it goes.' I said moving closer and taking the glass of wine from her hand and placing it on the mahogany night stand. I then took her face in both my hands and kissed her deeply, passionately. She grabbed my tongue hungrily and I began to feel the heat rise in me. I felt her remove my towel and insert me into her pulsating vagina. I drove my throbbing shaft into her warm, throbbing, vagina and felt her nails dig into my back as she gasped and clutched for anything available. Last night still fresh in my mind I made it a point to turn the music up to help mask her screams and I was glad I did.

'Finally,' Sivitra muttered loud enough for me to hear a smile plastered across her face.

'Finally what?' I asked never missing a beat.

'You finally came to your senses. Do you know how long I waited for you to come to your senses,' she said digging her nails into my shoulder. This time it was me who screamed. It was not long before she joined in. She was trying to slide from under me now.

'Oh my goodness! Oh shit! That's it! Oh shit baby! That's my spot! That's it! That's right. Fuck this pussy baby! Make it yours baby! Oh my goodness! Yes! That's it baby! I'm about to...'

'Is it good baby?'

'Oh yes, daddy. I'm about to...'

The more she talked the hotter and more passionate I became. I knew she was on the verge of climaxing when she arched her back and her hips left the bed. I felt the walls of her vagina and I knew she was about to come. Easing her back onto the bed I extricated myself. This time when she screamed it wasn't a scream of passion.

'What the hell are you doing?'

'Enjoying you.'

'Then why did you stop bay?'

I smiled as I sipped her wine and lit a cigarette.

'I'm sorry. I just didn't want it to end. I want to make love to you all night.'

'No you don't. I know exactly what you're trying to do Mr. Brown. You're trying to turn me out so I'll be just like the rest of your little chicken head fan club that follow you around and beg you to break them off every now and then.'

I had to smile. I liked her conspiracy theory. She had quite an imagination. Was this really her perception of me and other women.

'What are you smiling at?' she said still smiling. 'I'm right and you know it. That's why you're smiling isn't it?'

'Actually I'm smiling because I've never known anyone who in the middle of lovemaking stops to have a conversation instead of just savoring the moment.

'I guess I just like you Mr. Brown. The other time I had sex I just climbed under the cover and never said a word.'

'Lucky man,' I teased.

'Lucky girl,' she said smiling and pulling me into her once more.

Minutes passed and Sivitra was screaming again.

'Oh yes, daddy! You are good to me! You just tell 'Vitra what you want? Oh my God! Bert I think I'm coming sweetie! Please let me come this time?'

She was screaming loud enough now that I feared they could hear her two buildings down. I eased out before she came but to avoid her wrath I dropped down and kissed her inner thighs liberally until she began to moan and pull my head towards her vagina.

'Oh baby please. Baby please. Bert what do I have to do? Please don't tease me baby.' She was slapping the bed out of frustration before making a vain attempt to pull my head towards her throbbing vagina. When this didn't work she tried her best to slide down under my mouth. Then as if by cue she sat up and drained the rest of the bottle of Moscato.

'Are you going to give me what I want or am I gonna have to take it?'

I smiled saying nothing.

'Turn over and lay on your back.'

No sooner had I done this than Sivitra straddled my face with her pussy firmly pressed against my mouth. Spreading the lips to her vagina she fed me her treasures riding my face hard and fast. I sucked softly and gently on her hard and erect clitoris. She moaned long and loudly. The harder I sucked on her clit the louder she got After awhile there were no legible words. She was screaming now, one long continuous scream as she held fast to the headboard and ground her hips in my face. And even though her screams weren't legible I could hear her ask for solace, for a good man and a partner that would make her his priority, that she could trust and love freely, and who would make love to her just the way she was being made love to now. That's what I heard. It came from down deep in the darkest recesses of her mind this pain that she was releasing. When she came it was almost as if she had had an epiphany of sorts.

'Oh my goodness,' she giggled looking and smiling appreciatively. 'You're definitely a keeper. You know I've never done that before. I've always fantasized about a man catering to me and making me feel like a queen and Lord knows you took me there. I can't believe how intense that was. It was almost like an out-of-body experience. But my goodness you are really something Mr. Brown. Every man can't make a woman

feel the way I do right now. You have a special talent. That's a gift. I have to be careful. I could fall in love with just that,' she said closing her eyes and feigning sleep.

'Oh hell no. I know you don't think you're going to sleep.'

We made love 'til four or five in the morning. And I was glad that both my neighbors worked nights or else the cops would have been knocking. I spent the night taking her to the edge of an orgasm multiple times before coming to a complete stop. In that time she threatened me, promised me the world and proposed to me.

And although I would have absolutely loved to have been the heir apparent to Casanova I know that it wasn't my performance. I had no special God given talent. I just put her pleasure and satisfaction before all else.

All too often women are involved with men who have the 'me first' mentality in the bedroom. Usually objectifying women she becomes little more than a pleasure vessel. With the selfish attitude of 'I got mine get yours' the woman's needs are rarely met.

So, when someone of Sivitra's ilk walks into the life of one of these so-called men they often feel threatened by her tall, statuesque, frame which housed a gifted mind and a very real distrust of anyone promoting game.

We both had to work in the morning so I set the alarm clock for six which would give us time to beat the morning rush hour.

Now I thought I heard the alarm go off but I must have been dreaming. I turned over and went back to sleep. When I did wake up the clock read eight forty-seven.

Due there at nine I picked up the phone. Hell, I hadn't taken a day in nearly six months and I was exhausted.

'Morning David. This is Bert. Won't be coming in today. I have some personal matters I need to address.'

'No problem. I'll talk to you tomorrow.'

'Sweetheart. Do you see the time? I must have turned the alarm off. I thought I was hitting the snooze,' Sivitra said gathering the sheet around her naked frame and headed toward the bathroom. I grabbed her and turned her to face me.

'Sivitra. I just want you to know that before all this took place I thought you were wonderful but after last night I have to change that to amazing. You are truly amazing. I just want you to know that I'm a big fan.'

'Well thank you Mr. Brown but I did no more than follow your lead. I was just trying to keep up with the master. So, tell me Mr. Brown. Did I make the cut? Does Ms. Lighty get a day in Mr. Brown's calendar that can be hers and hers alone. I'm kind of fond of Sundays after yesterday. Sure wouldn't mind revisiting that day.'

I had to laugh.

'A day? I don't know what you don't get. I gave you a key. And don't get it twisted. That key works seven days a week. I want you to feel free to use it whenever you'd like.'

'Are you sure Mr. Brown?'

'Yes. I'm sure. I figure the more you use it the better chance I'll have of pushing Jake to the curb.'

'It's James,' she said smiling.

'Whatever.' I said feigning anger. 'He's in the way.'

'In the way? Don't you think you have quite enough to keep you busy without worrying about James?'

'You're right but I would certainly like to share a bigger part of your life.'

'I thought that's what we were doing. What we have is called friendship and it's good. I only wish I had had a relationship half as good as our friendship but let's keep it real love. We may care about each other and love each other but we're not in love with each other. Not yet anyway and that's kind of where you want to start a romantic relationship.'

'Enough said. I guess you clarified that.'

'Besides you haven't been free and single a year yet so I know you're not trying to link up with anyone and have the responsibility of having another ball-and-chain wrapped around your neck.'

'I'd hate to think of you in those terms but you're right.'

'Besides you haven't met all the women at Dorchester County. You may meet someone and fall head over heels in love. All I'm saying is give yourself a chance. I pray that doesn't happen but you deserve the chance to be happy.'

'I hear you.'

'Are you going to work?'

'No. I am exhausted. I called in earlier. What about you?'

'I'd like to stay right here in this same position forever.'

'Maybe not in that position,' I said grabbing her ankles and dragging her to the bottom of the bed.

'Baby please. You don't know how badly I want to revisit last night but I am so sore. It may take me the better part of a week to heal up. I've never been made love to like that before. It's usually, 'Wham! Bam! Thank you ma'm.' That's what usually happens. But last night you took me there twelve different ways. You were just so gentle and kind that I kept wanting to keep feeling that good. I couldn't get enough. Guess I was greedy. Now I'm feeling it. Still, kisses would be nice if you're of a mind to.'

'Oh, goodness. I think I 've created a monster.'

'Stop it. You make me sound like a nympho and I may be but I don't need you to announce it. Are you purposely trying to embarrass me?'

'Sorry sweetie. My bad,' I said taking her calves on my shoulders before I went for her tender delights. It was hours later when she passed out from what I deemed sheer exhaustion. Later she told me that she had come at least seven times and couldn't leave until she could reciprocate.

I let her know that that wasn't necessary. She then told me that she now knew how it felt to be a queen. She was going to call Jake just as soon as she got home and tell him she'd met someone else.

'He should have stepped up when he had the opportunity. He blew it. I am now an official member of the Bert Brown fan club. Shit. I'd wait on you hand and foot like Molly Maid if I could get that kind of treatment once or twice a week,' she said smiling.

'Molly Maid huh?'

'Molly Maid in my birthday suit baby.'

'Funny I was just thinking. If there's one thing I need it's a maid. But here's a proposition for you. Why don't you come and spend a couple of weeks and let me spoil you like the queen you are.'

'Oooh... That's very enticing. When are you talking?'

'What's wrong with today?'

'I don't know if that's a good thing or not. You're like a whirlwind, sorta like a tornado. And before you know it or can brace yourself you've swept me up. But Lord knows if I didn't get it before I get it now. I know why evil ass Alicia wouldn't or probably couldn't let go. And why I'm going to run home and come right back. I was told the worse thing in life is wasted potential and if I don't use the next two weeks to convince you that I am all the woman you'll ever need then I've wasted my own potential. Let me go before someone pinches me. I'll be back ,' she said kissing me on my cheek and closing the door behind her.

No sooner had she gone than the phone rang.

'I was just wondering. Can you take Friday off?'

'I don't know. I'll see tomorrow.'

'Do you work this weekend?'

'Unfortunately.'

'Don't say unfortunately. I'll be right next door.'

'That's true.'

'Okay love. I'll see you in a minute.'

Sitting behind the wheel of her new Ford Mustang and fixing her hair and her eyebrows before pulling off into the busy midday traffic Sivitra couldn't do anything but smile.

When she was long gone I sat down in the living room and thought about the past two days. Sivitra was right. We did not love each other but we did like each other very much. And we really enjoyed each other's company and conversation. But she was right. A romantic relationship would never work and yet I found myself excited about her return.

It would be fun playing house for two weeks but she was right. I did not want the added responsibility of a relationship. I had to focus. I missed my son and felt that I should be raising him but that was still some time away. His day care alone would cost me one of my paychecks and the rent and utilities all would have to come from my remaining check. No. I wasn't ready but I was moving in the right direction. I loved my son more than I loved life itself and wanted him more than I wanted anything. Thinking about all of this while Sivitra was gone the only thing I could think of was how to increase my pay so that I could have my son.

I had a plan. So, why she was gone I went to see Janet my supervisor to see if she could give me more hours.

'Good to see you Bert. It's been a while. I've been meaning to call a staff meeting if for no other reason than to keep my staff in touch with each other. And I'm the main culprit. I've been so busy I don't even get a chance to get out to the homes anymore. Let me make that my number one priority,' she said leaning back in the leather

captain's chair. 'I'm a need you to be my reminder. I want you to call me on Monday and tell me to set up a staff meeting. Can you do that?'

'Yes, ma'm.'

I liked Janet Springer, the director of Dorchester County Department of Mental Retardation and my supervisor. And it was apparent that she was quite fond of me one of only three male employees.

'I don't know what you're doing Bert but the word is getting around and all

I've been hearing are good things. And when I listen I know that half my ladies are in love with you. They say your name and their faces just light up. I'm not sure I know what you're doing to them and don't know that I want to know but whatever it is keep it up. You know you can move up quickly with the county. Just keep it up.'

'Thank you for the compliment Ms. Springer.'

'How many times do I have to tell you? It's Janet. You make me feel so old.'

'Sorry. It's just a term of respect.'

'I certainly would love to meet your parents. They certainly did a job on you.'

I smiled. If she only knew.

'They'll be here next month for the holidays.'

'I want to meet them. You call me when they get here. I would love to meet them so I can tell them what a job they've done.'

'I'll make sure I give you a call when they arrive.'

Janet Springer was a tall thin woman. I assumed she couldn't be anything but slim with her metabolism. She was constantly moving shaking things up and putting demands on herself and others. Perhaps her greatest asset was that she was a motivator. This was her gift. She was one of the few people I knew that could look at a person, size them up and map out a plan, an approach and through positive manipulation motivate that person to want to do her bidding. She was good. Damn good and she had my respect. She was not only bright, but witty. She was straightforward and honest but she could be brutal if you somehow took her kindness for weakness.

I can remember her picking out one particular staff member at a staff meeting for using one of the company vans for her own personal use. This was pretty much common practice and was downplayed or overlooked by Janet as long as all went well with our clients. Our clients remained our first priority and the reason we were in the county's employ.

'We are going to have to curtail our use of the vans for private usage and personal runs. I know the vast majority of you do not abuse this privilege. But most recently I had a staff member drop her clients off at the roller skating ring. The trip from that home to the roller skating has always been six miles but for some reason on this night the mileage log showed thirty six miles to and from the roller skating rink when it should have been twelve. To make it even worse the clients called me to tell me that she wasn't

there so I sent another staff member to the house to see if there was a problem. No one was there but when I called Phylicia told me that she had fallen asleep. That was after I sent someone to do a walk through of the house. But I don't want to belabor the subject. Please do not abuse staff privileges. Phylicia you may leave your keys and your badge at the front desk with security. You are no longer in our employ.'

I was shocked that she would fire an employee in front of her colleagues but in Janet Springer's mind the residents were our bread and butter and she was adamant that we were all on board with that. I wasn't okay with the way in which she fired Phylicia but I was committed to doing a good job and she could see my devotion so we got along quite well.

'What is it that I can do for you Bert?'

'You know I have a six year old son who lives with his mom?'

'Yes. You mentioned it.'

'Well, I would like to have him come and live with me but right now I'm barely making ends meet so I was wondering if there was another position, perhaps a supervisory position that was open.'

'No. Not at present but there should be at least two opening up in the next six months. This is between you and I. I'm about to do a major shake up. We have quite a few so-called staff members that are not particularly fond of their jobs so they will be leaving. I'll be bringing in some people who don't just see this as a job but are enthused

about providing a better quality of life for our clients. I hope not to have more than two vacancies at a time but I will need staff to cover those houses so you see once again you are a godsend. That is if you really are interested in doubling your hours.'

'I'm interested. I'm interested.'

'Beautiful. I can cross that one off my to do list. When would you like to start?'

'Just say the word.'

'Well, Phylicia's hours need to be picked up. She was scheduled to work the next two days. You work this weekend too. Don't you?'

'Yes ma'm.

'Okay. I don't want to do anything to pull you away from your guys. This is the first time since I've been here that we have some stability and I'm not getting phone calls either from that house or about that house.'

'It ain't easy,' I said matter-of-factly.

'I know it's not. I don't think I could do it. Billy alone would be enough to make me lose my job.'

'He's a handful alright.'

'And I thank you for taking care of him.'

'That's my job.'

'I wish I had more employees who thought like that. So, you'll be working eleven days straight. Are you okay with that?'

'That's fine.'

'I want you to be honest with me though. When you feel it's getting to be a bit too much I want you to call me and let me know.'

'Agreed.'

'What are you doing today?'

'I'm off today.'

'Oh okay. Good. I want you to meet someone. Have you met Tomasina?'

'No. I don't believe I have.'

'Seriously? You have to meet Tommy. She's another one of my super employees. Anyway, let me introduce you and then you can sit in on our little dilemma. Let me give you the skinny before I call them in.

I don't know if you're aware that one of your clients, Charles has a crush on Tomasina. You'll understand better after you meet her. You know he has his job at Po' Folks and he's been saving his money to take her out. The only problem I have with it is one of boundaries. Where Tomasina's concerned I don't think Charles has any sense of boundaries. He says he understands but he's only saying that for the sake of expediency but when it comes to Tommy he has no concept of client/staff relationship.

If you were to chaperone it would ease the pressure on Tommy and change the dynamics. I could approve that and dinner would be on the county tonight and you could pick up a couple of hours. You did say you wanted the extra hours didn't you?'

'That's fine.'

'And Bert I want you to know that I do appreciate this and I will do everything I can to get you in on one of the two positions I create.'

'Thank you Ms. Springer.'

'Janet and no I thank you. Now let me do the introductions,' she said standing and making her way to the door.

'Tommy, Charles come in and have a seat. Tommy this is Bert. He's been with us for close to a year I can't understand why you two haven't met.'

We hadn't met because I ran and hid every time I saw her. Five years older than I was at forty she was a handful. The fact that she was older and possibly wiser gave me pause. Still what made her spectacular in my eyes was her physical beauty. To this date I have never had the occasion to have known a more beautiful woman. Somewhere between a caramel and mocha she was perfectly proportioned with just a tad bit extra where a woman could stand a tad bit extra. To say she was one fine, thick redbone would be an utter disservice. I guess her greatest testament were the countless men who ignored the fact that I was her by her side to turn all the way around for a better view and a second look. These same men with their wives would turn full circle to look and pay homage. When I first glanced her I immediately conceded. There were levels and standards and when I first glanced Tomasina Alston I knew that I was not on her level. I was thoroughly intimidated even though she proved to be carefree and easy to talk to even if she knew

she was fine. She almost seemed to ignore it; going natural with her hair in a tight cropped afro and no make-up. Still, it did little to dismiss the wolf whistles and cat calls.

I'd done my homework when it came to Tomasina only to find out that she was the single mother of three teenage girls. Information was vague as to who the father was other than he'd been incarcerated for several years.

I'd no idea who my supervisor was referring to when she'd made the offer. Now it was too late to decline. I truly believed that Tommy was in a class by herself and a reach for me. Come to think of it I vaguely remember. I did meet her in passing but aside from her drop dead good looks I remember little. I remember running then. There was no running now.

It was around eleven when we got out of the meeting. Tomasina approached me no sooner than we got out.

'Never thought we'd need a chaperone on our first date,' she said smiling.

'I'm sorry. I told Janet I didn't trust myself alone with you.' I said smiling back.

'Is that right?'

'Told her just this morning.'

'Well, if that's the case then I guess that's the way it'll have to be at least for the time being. It is so hard trying to get you alone but then there's always tomorrow.'

'Wow. I didn't know. I've always been one to brake for beautiful women and you certainly fit that description.'

Tommy was grinning broadly.

'I say something funny?'

'No. It's just that I heard you were smmoth. They didn't lie. Can we continue this conversation tonight?'

'Looking forward to it.'

'Any suggestions as to where we should go?'

'I like the crab shack on Main.'

'Sounds good to me.'

'How's seven sound?'

'That's fine.'

'Good. Then I'll see you there.'

'Look forward to it.'

'Oh, and Tomasina it was nice to finally meet you.'

'My close friends call me Tommy and it was nice meeting you as well,' she said turning to go. I watched as she walked away. Lord knows she was one beautiful woman. Once home I called Sivitra to tell her that I would be working the rest of the week.

'No problem hon. I was just thinking. How would it feel to be around this man that I so desire yet not able to touch him or have him? So, I was hoping that I might be able to get a raincheck .'

'Whenever you're ready love. Tell me something though Sivitra. Who is this Tomasina Alston?'

'You know I keep to myself. I mean I worked withher once or twice. She seems really nice but it's hard to get a fix on who she really is because she keeps to herself I know she has three girls. But that's about it. She doesn't work a lot. I think she's in the church.'

'Thanks sweetie.'

'She really has you shook doesn't she?'

'No. Not at all. I signed up to escort she and Charles and I would like to know who I'm escorting. I've never spoken to her until today. I always thought she was in a different league. And I just assumed she was arrogant and sort of stuck on herself. That's my perception.'

'It might be but you have her pegged all wrong but I'm not going to say anything. Seeing is believing. But on the real she's very nice. Just don't let her be too nice to you. I have plans for you.'

I laughed.

'I'm not joking Bert. I've waited way too long. And if I know women she set this whole thing up. She probably told Janet that she didn't feel comfortable being alone with Charles. Trust me she knows that you work with Charles and probably said she'd feel better if she had a third person along. I'd be willing to bet you she arranged the whole thing. But I ain't worried about her. I'm worried about you. You call me as soon as you get home.'

'I'll do that sweetheart.'

'Are you nervous?'

'I guess you can say that.'

'Listen. Pour yourself a double, say fuck it and eat all the crabs you can eat. Everything else will fall into place. And Bert. Do me a favor and wear a condom just in case something should kick off.'

'I gotcha. I'll talk to you later sweetie.'

The crab house was across the street from my apartment so I walked. I felt the Jack Daniels coursing through my veins and wasn't nearly as nervous as I had been. That was until Tommy walked in in a white Marilyn Monroe dress and white heels. No. I was not ready for this, for her and headed for the bar.

'Give me a double of Jack and a beer chaser,' I said peeking at Tommy from behind a stone pillar. I threw the drinks down and headed for the table.

'You look very nice tonight Tommy,' I said my eyes never leaving Tommy.

'Well thank you. You don't look too bad yourself Mr. Brown.'

Not to be outdone Charles chimed in.

'I know. I've been saving this shirt for a special occasion and I consider Tommy a special occasion. Wouldn't you agree Bert?'

'Absolutely Charles. A date with Tommasina is definitely a special occasion. Any man would count himself as lucky to have a date with her,' I said my eyes never leaving Tommy.

The three of us sat and talked and laughed about all kinds of things. I found Tommy to be warm and down-to-earth. And when it was over and Charles stood by Tommy's car we chatted with me inviting her over for a night cap after she took Charles home.

Fifteen minutes later I heard her pull up and her car door slam. I could tell she was already tipsy when she arrived. I suggested her spending the night but she declined saying she had to get home to her girls and then with a quickness I have yet to see before or since Tomasina Alston stripped naked. I followed her lead and an hour later I sat in the living room listening to Sade, sipping some wine and revisiting what had just transpired. I'd just made love with the most beautiful girl in the world and I was clueless.

I knew why I had. Tommy was out of my league. She was gorgeous. She was bright. She was not only mature but wise. And she was attracted to me for some reason. Now I must admit that that may be a bit shallow but the fact that she was older and beautiful were the primary reasons. The next day I woke up refreshed with a new lease on life. It was close to nine o'clock and once again I took the time to relive each moment of the night before.

An hour or so later there was a knock at the door. It could only be one person. Sivitra. Everyone else had learned not to stop by without calling.

'So how did it go sweetie?'

'Charles had a ball. He was in heaven.'

'You know good and well I could care less about Charles. How was it for you?'

'I took your advice and had a double before I left and another one when I got there.'

'So, you were feeling no pain?'

'None whatsoever but I really didn't need it. I was totally off. She was nothing like I thought and I actually enjoyed her conversation. I thought she'd be stuck up and bourgie but she was the salt of the earth.'

'Stop being naive. Stop underestimating women. They all have a hidden agenda.'

'I hear ya.'

'Good. Now let's cut through the chase and down to the nitty gritty. Did you sleep with her?'

I smiled as I tried to gather my thoughts.

'No. But listen baby if some woman asked me if I slept with you do I have the right to share your business?'

'That's not the same. You've told me every woman you've slept with so far. Now all of a sudden you can't tell me.'

'You're right. We were friends before. You were my confidante so yes I told you but now that we are trying to be an item the only thing we can talk about is you and I. There are no other women or interests until I see where we end up. Right now I'm only interested in seeing how far you and I can go.'

'You are truly the last of a dying breed. Most brothas would have been like, yeah I slept with the bitch or yeah I fucked the bitch. I ain't tryna do nothin' with it though. She married. But damn I might have to hit that shit agin. She got a fat ass and some good pussy.'

I smiled.

'Anyway I know that you slept with her.'

'And why do you see that?'

'Your whole demeanor has changed. You're more upbeat and alive than I've seen you in a long time.'

'And why can't that be because you're here. You know you make my everyday brighter.'

'It could be but I think the used condom on top of the trash may have more to do with your upbeat attitude than my presence.'

I was speechless. Needless to say we didn't make love that day. Come to think of it I don't think we made love again although we remained close.

Tomasina was like a whirling devilish upsetting the uneasy balance in my life. At first, her showing up unexpectedly was a nice touch but I began to notice that if I had company and she showed up they would defer to her and leave. She commanded that type of respect. And I have yet to see her do anything but smile and be cordial. Still, her presence spoke otherwise. And once she made it known that she had her sights set on me my visits ceased altogether.

We never spoke about other people or the fact that I was single and dating. That was a moot point as she assumed every role in my life including wife and lover. A pretty good cook in my own right I can't recall cooking after we met. I especially enjoyed Fridays when she would stop by the fish market and pick up a couple of pounds of croakers and porgies and a six pack of beer. She'd fry fish and we'd eat and sip beer and listen to Will Downing until the wee hours of the morning.

About a month or two following our first date I noticed that my entire lifestyle had been altered. As I mentioned early the word had somehow gotten out that I was seeing Tommy and all interest in me ceased.

It was interesting since we made it a point to be discreet and were seldom seen in public. What time we spent together we spent indoors. With three teenage daughters and a nephew that suffered some type of debilitating illness which had him hooked up to a host of machines she had little time for anything other than me and her own household. Tommy would take care of home which was a twenty four job and then come visit me as a sort of respite.

I slowly came to know her. What seemed to make her happiest was cooking and watching television. My expectations and drives came to a crashing halt. It took even less to satisfy me. I was in heaven just knowing someone of her ilk would have anything to do with me. I had no idea what was on her mind or what the attraction was where she was concerned. The only motive I saw her having was to take me off the market and claim me for her very own because she could. This moved elevating her and establishing her as the matriarch of all that was Dorchester County Department of Retardation. I had no objection. I readily accepted the fact that she filled in all the voids and added a woman's touch to my mundane life.

She took a particular interest in my apartment as well. She looked for no applause or credit. If she saw a need she filled it. It was nothing to come home to matching shower curtains, rugs and other accessories that turned my standard bathroom into a showcase for Better Homes and Gardens. It was the same with the kitchen. Farm animals suddenly became the modem. I was grateful and thanked her. She didn't work a

lot. Nor did she have a lot and seemed to have reconciled herself with that fact and was at peace with herself. There were times when she would wish for things and I would tell her that God helps those who help themselves but she would simply reply that she could do without as God wouldn't allow her to do that at this juncture in time. I left it alone.

She never cried over money but I knew that having three teenage daughters and a nephew on life support she was just making ends meet and yet here she was contributing to my household at every turn.

Months passed and I had to admit that I was glad for Tomasina bringing some stability to my life. Since she'd become apart of my life I saw no need to go out. Eventually I saved enough money to go and get my son although I wasn't exactly sure how that was going to work out being that I lived in an adults only community. Still, I was ready and Tommy did her best to assure me that all would be fine. And with her assurance I knew the transition for Chris and myself would be that much smoother. But something still bothered me.

What was her motive? Was Sivitra right? Did she have ulterior motives? We had never discussed our relationship although by this time I was head over heels in love with this woman. Still, and as much time as she spent with me I still wondered where her feelings lay.

She never did say but I could assume from all the attention she showered on me that she must be sharing similar feelings. We spent every waking hour together when we

weren't working we chilling and talking and sipping wine before returning to the bedroom where she did her best to keep me both happy and satisfied. Oh, how I loved this woman.

I drove to Fayetteville, North Carolina after she convinced me that all would be fine with my bringing my son into the fold. So, convincing was she that I left the Friday afternoon after work to go to Fayetteville to go pick up Chris. I returned Saturday morning to find my guest room transformed into a little boy's bedroom complete with Barney posters and pictures of race cars. He was tickled. No sooner had we gotten back Tommy sent her oldest daughter to pick him up. I did not see her or my son anymore that weekend. He must have been treated extremely well because every other word was Ms. Tommy said this and Ms. Tommy did that. From what I understand the girls fought for his attention all weekend.

I hardly saw my son in the months to follow. And when the school notified me that there was no bus pick up located near me as I was in an adults only community

Tommy was there at six thirty to take him to the day care which would then transport him to his school.

All was well and I couldn't have been happier with the arrangement and all that Tommy was doing and was on the verge of asking her to marry me when Sivitra's warning came to mind.

'Don't underestimate her. She has her own agenda.'

Not only did she have her own agenda unbeknownst to me but she also had three daughters and a nephew on life support. In addition to what I mentioned she was married and living on her in-her laws land. I dared not delve into her relationship and feelings towards her estranged husband. She, on the other hand, never mentioned him once.

As my father used to say, 'Never look a gift horse in the mouth.' So, I continued our relationship as if nothing had changed hoping that in due time she would want to proceed further with our relationship. And being that there were no riffs and I depended heavily on her I let it go even though I still had questions.

In the meantime, Tommy spent her every waking hour with Christopher more or less adopting him and making him her own. When she wanted to spend some time alone with me she would call her daughters to see if they wanted to babysit. They were there in the next ten to fifteen minutes vying to see who he would go to.

It's a funny thing though. I have no recollection of us having sex or making love after the initial time. What we had was so much more than that although she was always a willing participant when it was time to join me in the bedroom. We were sharing life and were so busy setting an example and raising children that we could hardly breathe.

Tomasina forced me into being not a good parent but a great parent along

with being a role model and a stellar employee. Her mantra was 'Strive for excellence. If you fail you can always settle for greatness.'

She made me a better person and I was appreciative. I enjoyed her company and was content if not pleased with life in general. If there had been a void in my life she filled it. Suddenly, there was no need to run, to date, to sleep with women. I had finally found everything and more in Tomasina. She completed me and made me whole.

The Christmas holidays were rapidly approaching although was hard to tell by the weather in South Carolina. My father who I must say is very traditional in his thinking when it comes to matters such as family called me on several occasions during this time. I knew he missed his buddy and shadow and was contemplating coming to visit over the Christmas holidays. I loved my father and was glad to have him come. It was important that he see how well I was doing. I knew he was

proud of me if for no other reason than raising my son. As the good son I went all

out to make sure he had

everything possible to make his stay comfortable. I mentioned his visit in passing

to Tommy who seemed elated to meet my father.

Upon his arrival Tommy picked him up from the train station. By the time he

arrived at the house they were the best of friends. I do believe my father fell in

love with her almost as quickly as I did and for many of the same reasons.

'She's a stallion,' he commented when she left. 'You be careful when it comes to

a woman like that.'

I wasn't really sure what I was supposed to be careful about but he wasn't the first

person to tell me that about her so I heeded his advice not to mention that my

father had always had my best interest at heart. A literate man he was always

cautious to a fault, (some may even say slightly paranoid), but his caution had

served him well in his era where a lack thereof could have easily cost him his life.

He understood people and the system we found ourselves in and he always reacted appropriately and accordingly and was never involved in anything other than being aware. He tried to impart this on me but I was still somewhat naive especially when it came to matters of the heart. My father feared for both his son and grandson. I guess he just had an inkling.

I've always loved my father dearly. To this day I remain his protege and he remains my mentor and idol. As long as I've known him his family's welfare always came first and foremost. Now he was showing concern. Something was definitely bothering him but if I know my father, (and I do), he would never tell me anything for

fear that he may be interfering in a place where he had no business. Perhaps this was as much as he could share with me. His suspicion raised doubt in mind. This was the first time in close to a year of being together that I had some reservations about her.

That night we sat around the dinner table and discussed the upcoming day. I had to work and Chris was in school leaving my father at home all alone.

'I'm not working tomorrow. I can come pick you up in the morning and give you a tour of Charleston if you like?'

I have to admit I was a little shocked but then that's just who Tommy was. I rationalized it by putting a game face on and acknowledging that that's what partners did. And I couldn't have asked for a better one. Anyway that's how I rationalized it when actually I looked at it with a tinge of jealousy. Why was my woman availing herself to another man without at least discussing it with me to see how I felt or didn't my feelings and opinions come into play? Sure, he was my father and that's what bothered me even more. He had a long history of being a philanderer and I don't know if he ever saw a woman who he didn't like.

The following morning Tommy was there bright and early to pick Chris up and drop him off at day care. I was still getting dressed when she appeared at the bathroom door in the shortest mini-skirt. More thigh showed than was covered. I was appalled thinking her dress was quite inappropriate to be taking my father out in. I wanted to say something and probably should have but I wasn't sure if I were jealous and my comments would only confirm that I neither believed she or my father to be morally correct. That would have been an awful accusation. I never said anything but my father's visit changed our relationship. My own insecurities always wondered what happened that day.

And then my father did something that was really out of character for him. I went Christmas shopping and bought every book I had an inkling he was interested in. Then I tried to clothe him from head-to-toe. I spent the better part of the night wrapping and placing them under the tree along with gifts for Chris' and Tommy's. I even had gifts for my three newly adopted daughters.

On Christmas morning I woke even more excited than six year old Chris. I loved playing Santa Claus and knowing that I'd had some hand in making them smile. When the three of us had gathered and I'd distributed all the gifts my father called me to the front window.

'Now you don't have to depend on anyone,' he said pointing to the brand new cherry red Pontiac in the parking lot below. Grateful was not the word for how I felt but what was even more apparent was the fact that my father put twenty five hundred dollars down on a car to let me know I was in dangerous waters. He never said a word but I got the message loud and clear. What was it that he knew that he didn't want to tell me? Had it been that bad?

He left not long after Christmas and called to tell me he arrived home safely and to thank me.

'You know Tomasina was telling me that her oldest daughter was trying to get into college so I gave her my number if she wanted me to write a reference letter.

Her daughter called me to ask me if she could borrow two thousand dollars.'

'No, she didn't.' I said incredulously.

This was all a bit hard for me to fathom. I knew all three girls and I knew that none of the three would have ever thought to approach a stranger without their mother's prodding.

As soon as I hung up with my father I called Sivitra.

'Can you believe that?'

'It's hard to believe that she would have the gall to do something like that and I'd be willing to bet that you still don't know what her overall agenda is.'

'Don't have a clue but I would never have expected her to solicit money from my father. She just met him. That kinda hurts.'

'I guess it would. But hold up. Pause for a second. Weren't you the one that warned me about putting all my eggs in one basket? I know you're hurt but you can stop the bleeding and cut your losses before it gets any worse. I wouldn't even worry about it if I were you.'

'And why is that?'

'There's too many lonely women out here just waiting for a good brotha to come along. In fact, I know this cute little chick. I think she's a senior at Charleston Southern and she's just waiting for the green light so she can show you how a good man is supposed to be treated.'

I had to smile.

'I'll keep that in mind sweetie but right now I've got to work this out first. I should just walk away. There's really no need for any further conversation.'

'That's the right thing to do. But that's the hardest thing to do after all this time. You're gonna have to work your way through this and the only thing that will heal this is time. But you're gonna need closure before you can walk away. Especially when you're in love. You want to know why she would do anything to upset your happiness. Wasn't she happy? You thought you were moving forward together until this. Why didn't she come to you first and discuss it? And trust me these are just some of the questions you want answered. Did she ever love you? You need to know but see I'm going to tell you like you tell me. If your heart hadn't been involved and emotions were at a minimum you wouldn't have second thoughts about losing her number but no you got caught up and fell in love. You can't just say two 'tears in a bucket and say fuck it.' You're caught up and there's a good chance you're gonna get hurt far worse hanging around tryna get some answers that maybe are better left unsaid.'

'I hear you. I've got to extricate myself with the quickness. This is not who I am. I'm searching for peace and tranquility. Anyone bringing drama has to go.'

'I hear you and just hope it's that easy. This ain't Sharon or Alicia. You have feelings for this woman. This is a horse of a different color. Just take your time and follow your head and not your heart. Just remember. If it doesn't feel right it probably ain't right.'

'I hear you baby. I'll keep you posted.

The days that followed my father's leaving were full of animosity although I did my best to mask it when Tommy was around. I had so many questions and I began to detach myself. Taking a step back I began to notice that there was something definitely askew when it came to this woman. For months now I had begun to contemplate her worth in my life. More and more I came to believe that I was driven to the extent that excess was barely enough. I wanted to progress in every facet of my life and my partner had neither the aspiration or drive to do anything other than producing children that she could ill afford to take care of.

I, on the other hand, wanted to be married and live a rather unencumbered and simple life with my equal who also felt the passion and desire that drove me. We could teach and motivate each other in our quest for excellence.

But as I said Tommy had little or no aspirations and refrained from working as much as possible and yet would ask my father for money. I cannot recall her saying 'I love you' or ever discussing the possibility of marriage. To me the mere discussion of marriage meant there was some growth and possibility for the future. But there was no talk of marriage or anything else of relevance and we soon fell into a mundane existence. Our relationship had grown stagnant. I wanted to call Sivitra but I'd been faithful up until this point and if something were to grow awry I wanted it said that I was not the reason. And even though I was seriously debating our relationship I knew this was not the proper way to end it The truth of the matter was that I had no reason to hurt Tommy. As troubled as I was the fact of the matter was that I still loved this woman.

It remained so for the next month or so when she rented a car to drive up for my sister's wedding. I was so starved for her admission of love that I took this as a sign that we were good again and back in the fold.

The day we left she wore a tight blue jean dress that accentuated her more positive attributes. When we stopped for gas I noticed more than one gentlemen turning completely around to get a second look at this perfectly sculptured physical specimen. And though I was proud to have her by my side the die had been cast.

Tommy was well received at home. My mother was amazed at the rapport between she and Chris with him often going to her and putting his head in her lap when he was tired or upset. But then she'd always been kind and gentle with him and they had bonded almost immediately. And everyone that knew the family knew that once my mother, the matriarch of our family had signed off on you you were good to go.

Tommy was in. The men adored her for obvious reasons and she worked the crowd easily with her grace and charm moving in and out of small circles leaving everyone feeling better for having met her. To say she cemented a place among my family was an understatement. Well, that is she cemented a permanent place with everyone except my father who was still skeptically opposed and adamant as he could be without voicing an opinion but I knew.

I left feeling so proud that I once again contemplated forcing our relationship to the next level and letting the chips fall where they may. I considered all of this on the ride home. When we arrived three hours later I begged her to spend the night. I brought the luggage up while Tommy put Chris to bed. We were a good couple. Perhaps I was just too critical. I made love to Tomasina to the wee hours of the morning doing my best to please her. I was putting the full court press on, stepping my game up. I just wanted her to entertain the idea of marriage. All she had to do was allude to it and I'd sell her on the idea. That was my intent.

There was no better time to put my plan in motion than Valentine's Day which was the following day. Monday morning Valentine's Day I woke up. I had ordered a dozen roses from the local florist about a week ago so I headed there to pick up

Tommy's. Once delivered I planned on taking her to breakfast before heading to work.

At seven thirty I pulled up in front of her old beaten up trailer that she called home. Her daughter came to the door. I was ready to run in the way I usually did but Kendra's face told me that something was off kilter.

'I don't think it's a good time Mr. Bert.'

'What's wrong Kendra?' I said sticking my head and looking down the hall to Tommy's bedroom. I saw a man with his arm wrapped around my Tommy. I jerked back as if I'd just been hit. And in a way I guess I had. Here was my Tommy in bed with another man.

'My dad's home.' Kendra muttered.

I turned and headed for the car roses still in hand.

Ms. Wright

I have to admit that the aforementioned events left me devastated and as much as I loved Charleston the memories were too much for me to live with. So, I picked up and moved back to North Carolina. Only this time it was Greensboro, the home of the Civil Rights Movement and the home of two of the finer historically Black colleges.

I now had a daughter with my son's mother. She always acted as my rock when something terrible would happen and because she loved me would always have the compassion to take me back. I loved both my children dearly and loved their mother as well but we were no longer in love but were doing the right thing in raising our children together. At least it was the honorable thing to do. It wasn't hard since Cheryl and I were and had always been the best of friends. We were good parents and better together than we were trying to do it alone. So, our union was at best a matter of convenience. She was a simple woman content with a forty ounce of beer and a can of oysters. I wanted more.

We moved to Greensboro, to an apartment, sight unseen. I immediately began my search to sell my wares even before I sought a job. We needed quick money to get our lives up and running and off the ground so I began to search for the nearest flea market. A couple of years had passed since I'd made fifty two thousand dollars working two days a week at the flea market. It was profitable and gave you a nice cushion once I

found regular employment. By now I had become quite astute at buying used but relatively high end pieces and reselling them at close to brand new prices.

The tables outside, surrounding the flea market were ten dollars a table and required you to be there at five o'clock in the morning to get one. I didn't mind getting up at the crack of dawn since potential earnings could be upwards of a thousand dollars on a good day. And Saturday's were usually good not that the flea market was that big but the clientele came from Virginia, (which was no more than fifteen minutes away), and Greensboro and surrounding areas.

The way it evolved was Africans and Americans were up front selling new items like Nikes and Timberland boots and all the latest in urban fashion. I fit in well and quickly carved out both a niche and a loyal clientele. I sold brand new brass vases, elephants and other brass accessories. I also sold African American art, music and literature and women's clothing.

I ran into a bit of flak about my selling music. A white fellow who picked out a corner spot in the very back of the flea also sold music and felt my and complained to the owner. 'There's a Black fellow selling Black music and it's hurting my business.' Now the owner was a good ol' boy. A red-neck if I'd ever seen one and he established the policy that there could be no more than two vendors selling the same thing and up until arrived there had been only one music man. Now there were two. So, what was the problem? The problem is that Dennis had held a monopoly on the music business in the

flea until I arrived. But that was not the problem as I saw it. The problem that bothered me was that this man thought that he had some inalienable right to sell Black music, to exploit us further but didn't think that I should or was qualified to sell it. It was an interesting concept. A white man feels entitled to sell and profit off of Black culture but we should not and cannot be allowed to do that for which we created. The white man sure does have an interesting way of thinking when it comes to Black folks. I continued to sell my music and he continued to complain.

I was too valuable to the owner for him to take the complaints seriously and would simply parlay my neighbor's displeasure with me selling music and eating into his profits. But and although the owner carried a gun in plain view there were still heated disputes. Typically if the dispute was between two vendors and he would call on my services to mediate the dispute and find some common ground. He and I agreed on the fact that a dispute which ended any way other that than amicably hurt the flea market and in turn hurt everyone's pockets. So, I had this face, on the one hand, and I brought in a nicer, more subdued class of Negroes which only added to the flea market. The fact was that I brought people in and expanded the flea market. So, he was adverse to saying anything to me. Most of my wares I sold in my booth inside. The hotter items, the quick sellers went outside where the majority of the traffic was.

At the time I was also working for a company that graded elementary school student's writing tests. I didn't particularly like the job. It was nothing if not monotonous but the salary was good and it afforded a good deal of flexibility which I took full advantage of. I told them in the beginning that I owned my own business and would not be able to work Fridays so they allowed me to work four ten hour days instead.

On Fridays I went shopping for the flea market and soon began selling women's dresses and suits. Goodwill, thrift stores and yard sales were my wholesale distributors. I met with surprising success in my new venture. Of course there were other benefits to shopping women's clothes. One was that a women's clothier almost always attracted women and that was always a good thing.

This Saturday was turning out to be a particularly good one financially and it was unusually busy. Money was flowing and the overall atmosphere was good. My music was playing and Sam Cooke was crying a 'Change is Gonna Come' when three middle-aged women approached. They were all brown skin and attractive. You could look and see that they had all been stunners in their hey day. The eldest and most outspoken of the three looked at me and smiled.

"I came by here last week with my brother-in-law to pick up a CD from you but I guess we missed you. Hold on. I have it written down," she said rummaging through her bag for the song. "Here it is. He wants the Clarence Carter CD with Strokin' on it."

I went over to the CD rack and pulled the requested music and handed it to her. She smiled then leaned over and whispered this.

"Where do you get your dresses? The Goodwill?" she asked.

'Oh, no you didn't.'

I knew she was just picking, trying to get my goat, and making her best attempts to flirt. She was like a little grade school girl who doesn't know how to tell little Bobby Ray that she likes him so she throws rocks at him to get his attention and eventually puts his right eye out. The way she was hurling insults I recognized that she did not know how to express what it was that she liked and wanted. It was okay though. I wasn't intimidated in the least and was by this time pretty adept at reading the signs.

I caught up with her outside browsing. We walked and talked and in that time I found out she'd only recently been widowed. She had three children. Her oldest was her son who had his own law practice in Charlotte. A daughter who was mistering in either Raleigh or Durham. And her baby Corey who was still at home and in high school. Seems she was from a small town about an hour south of Fayetteville known as Elizabethtown. She'd left there after high school to attend all girls, Bennet College where they graduate elegance and class. Myrtle portrayed the best of both. She'd married and remained in Greensboro ever since.

She looked extremely good to be fifty some odd years old and talking to her for a few minutes it became obvious that good looks wasn't all that she possessed. She was not only a bright woman but politically astute as well. She intrigued me.

"What are you doing after you finish up here at the flea market?"

"My friend Andy allows me to post up outside of his Chinese Restaurant on Cone."

"You're quite the little entrepeneur. Aren't you?"

"Just tryin' to keep the lights on," I responded.

"So, what time do you expect to finish?"

"I don't know. I guess somewhere between six or seven."

"How 'bout I swing by and scoop you up around six-thirty?"

"I'll be there," I said coolly hoping not to sound too anxious."

At promptly six-thirty I saw the navy blue Mercedes Benz pull up. I'd made somewhere in the neighborhood of eight or nine hundred for the day when she showed up so I didn't mind leaving. She touted a blue floral dress and a pair of navy blue mules. Stepping out of the car I was shaken. She was a stunning woman.

"You need help packing up?"

"No. I'm good. Give me about ten minutes," I said as I broke the table down and packed it away.

Now I usually get a few butterflies anytime I go out on a first but today was different. Minutes later I sat in the front seat with her. Reaching under the seat she handed me a bottle of Hennessey.

"Want to go to Harper's up at Friendly?"

"Sounds good." I didn't know much about the place. I'd stopped in on occasion but it wasn't one of my regular watering spots for a number of reasons. But primarily because it was up scale and rather pricey.

We went and had more than a few drinks. An hour later we were both lit.

"Oh. That's not bad," she said before handing her card to the waitress.

"I can take that," I volunteered.

"You can pick it up tomorrow night."

"I guess that means that I'm going to see you tomorrow night?" I asked.

"I'm sorry. I didn't mean to be so presumptuous. I should have said that you can pick up the tab the next time we go out if there is a next time. I probably should have asked if you would like to go out again. Would you?"

"Absolutely. But I would like to have a say in the time and the place."

"Oh, okay. I'll wait for you to call and ask me then."

We were both a little tipsy when we left Harpers. It was close to ten o'clock and after telling her how much I enjoyed her company I made my way to my car. By the time I reached my car Myrtle was pulling up next to me. Putting the window down she beckoned me to her.

"Yes ma'am."

"Corey just called me to say he's staying at a friend's house. Would you like to come over for a night cap?"

I smiled. I guess she felt as I did and didn't want the night to end. I liked her even though I often felt like a novice when we spoke of politics and under things. Still, I had no objection to learning if she were willing to teach me. I knew a woman of her stature had the power to have whatever she wanted. She had access to a number of means. She could use her good looks and feminine wile or she could use her financial means to procure whatever it is that she desired. To me that was power.

It was at this time that I came to find out that one of the premier soul food restaurants and one of A&T's mainstays was a little restaurant called The Summit Cafe. My family and I would frequent the tiny restaurant every time we visited Greensboro for fish and grits. My mother, a restaurant owner in her own right and the owner hit it off right away. He was a nice sort of fellow and we got along well. Now I was inches away from fucking his wife.

In conjunction with the restaurant Myrtle owned three furniture stores in her own right. What most people don't know is that North Carolina is the furniture capitol of the world. Myrtle learned the furniture business and was teaching me. She would drive up to Hickory every Friday and buy wholesale and then stock her own store with furniture purchased a day or so prior. The markup was better than a hundred per cent and she couldn't keep enough furniture in stock.

Between her looks and financial prowess there was very little that Myrtle couldn't procure which in turn only increased her smugness. I don't believe she was intentionally arrogant and smug but with all of her attributes entwined I'm guessing this was the sum total. Much of what people saw was the way in which she carried herself. She was bright, yet quiet and aloof. It gave others the appearance that she didn't care or wasn't interested in them as people as human beings. Truth was she didn't see and didn't care. She wasn't interested in anything other than the empire she was building for herself. I liked this about her. She was driven from within and her only and toughest competition was none other than herself. The only problem was that I was also spoiled and arrogant to a degree and wasn't about to cow-tow to any of her whims. In truth I had already begun to without being aware. She was both shrewd and cunning and sought to draw me into the web she was spinning. Not knowing her motive and afraid of getting caught up in another misadventure I declined her invitation for a nightcap as much as I wanted her.

The next day I did everything I could not to call her but her subtle allure and witty conversation had added so much to my life giving it the vitality it was lacking that I gave in and called to see what her plans were for the evening.

"Was hoping you would call? What's up?" She said the energy emanating with every word and I knew she was excited. What she didn't know was as much as I tried to downplay it I was feeling the same way.

"Nothing really. Just wanted to hear your voice is all."

"You know you can be quite sweet when you want to be."

"I want to be."

"Then why don't you meet me at Monte Cristo's on Tower and Market. I have a taste for Mexican. I still have some of that Hennessey left. We can stop by the house for that night cap you turned down last night."

"Give me a time. I'm in Reidsville now but give me forty-five and I'll meet you there. Go ahead and order. I just ate a little while ago."

"Okay. By the way, how did you do today?"

"It was okay. Typical Monday. A few hundred."

"Okay. I have a proposition for you."

"I'm listening."

"I'll tell you when I see you."

"See you soon."

I wondered what type of proposition she had in mind. I wondered if it was a legit business proposition or was she just trying to secure a partner for her more immediate concerns. There was only one way to find out.

An hour later I pulled into the parking lot of Monte Cristo's and adjusted my clothes before going in. Up until this time there had been no physical contact but I had a feeling that tonight would be different. Walking in I saw a waiter trying to make conversation in a vain attempt to get her number all to no avail. She was sipping a double of something brown when I approached the table.

"Jose this is my date. Bert. Jose."

The waiter looked me up and down in utter disdain as he walked away.

"Hey, Myrtle," I said leaning over and kissing her lightly on the cheek.

"Good to see you too. What are you having to drink?"

"Whatever you're having is fine."

"Jose would you mind bringing Mr. Brown a double Jack."

"That's okay. I need to use the rest room. I'll order it from the bar on my back," I said sliding out of the booth. I didn't want Jose bringing me anything.

When I returned Myrtle reached across the table and holding both my hands in hers whispered to me.

"I have a proposition you might be interested in."

"I'm listening."

"I know you've heard that Carolina Circle Mall is being transformed into a flea market."

"I've heard."

"Well, I was thinking about selling furniture there. I want you to run it. You can sell sand in a desert. I think you would be perfect. You can branch out and sell CD's and DVD's up front and find someone to work the other flea market and I'm going to write you an incentive check for start up money."

"Interesting proposition. When do you need an answer?"

"As soon as you decide but don't cash the check until you've decided to come on board."

I smiled as I glanced down at the check for fifteen hundred.

"What's so humorous?"

"I'm sorry and I don't mean to sound ungrateful. I am grateful for the incentive and that you have such faith in me but I do okay by myself and am not ready to expand. I don't know if you've noticed or not but it's just me. Now if you could increase the manpower it would sound so much more appealing. If you haven't noticed I 'm already overwhelmed."

"Well, tell me then what would it take to get you on my team?"

"I'm not sure but I learned a long ago not to volunteer for anything."

Myrtle was having none of this. Snatching the check she ripped it up and wrote another and slid it across the table. I looked at it and smiled.

"This is my final offer. I'll give you until tomorrow to come to a decision."

"Or?"

"Or I rescind my offer. But let's not jump the gun just yet. Meet me at the car when you finish with Jose," she said sliding out the door her thick caramel thighs telling me to get on board. She wore no stockings or panty hose and her calves glistened like gargoyles in the midday sun. And if what I thought was about to happen was the deal clincher then perhaps the two grand in addition now offered was not such a bad deal after all. Lord knows she turned me on in the physical sense.

I could have given her the answer right then and there but I wanted her to sweat a little before I committed. I wanted her to know that her good looks and money could not affect me. Two thousand was a paltry sum but a much needed one.

Reaching the car I found Myrtle sitting there putting on her lipstick. I got in. Her dress halfway up her thigh I was again aroused. I admit I was weak.

And then as if by cue knowing she had all but broken me she lifted her blouse and unbuckled her bra and allowed her speckle breast to fall freely. She than grabbed me by the back of my head and held it firmly against her breast.

"Taste it. Lick it. Suck it. Ohh baby..."

And then just as quickly she pulled her arms out of the bra, she pulled her blouse down and started the car. Five minutes later we pulled up in front of her rather palatial home. Guiding me into the house and then the living room where she let her skirt fall revealing no underwear. Her body resembled that of a thirty year old. I marveled at how well she'd kept.

"Where are your underwear?" was the best I could do as I stared fixated on the body before me.

"Took them off when I was on the phone with you. Started to get warm. And wanted to make it easier on you if you had a mind to," she said winking at me. "Then again I didn't realize what it took to tempt you. I obviously don't get it done for you. What is it? Am I too old for you?"

"Now where did that come from. You know I'm attracted to you. Here I am lying in the middle of the living room floor naked from the waist down and... But you're right I am distracted. I keep wondering when Corey's going to walk in and see me trying to hump his mother. Wonder what his reaction will be? So, yeah I wouldn't say I'm actually comfortable. And why am I here naked from the waist down? I guess it's because you don't get it done for me. Now come here so I can put all doubt out of your mind and show you how I really feel about you."

I felt her come two or three times before Corey was due home and we called it a night.

"Can we pick up where we left off tomorrow night," she asked smiling contentedly.

"I don't know. Tomorrow is hectic for me. I do yard sales in the morning. If you like you can go with me."

"What time do you do yard sales?"

"I like to be at the first one no later than seven. I'm usually finished by mid day."

"If you'd said nine I would probably would have agreed but I'll just be rolling over good at seven. Why don't you stop by when you get through with the yard sales."

"I suppose I can stop by and see what's on the menu," I said winking at her.

"Goodnight, Mr. Brown."

Getting in the car I smiled and waved at the half naked frame still standing in the doorway. On the way home I was still smiling. My thoughts were scattered. Here I was poor as Joe's turkey, out here in the streets everyday hustling bootleg CD's and DVD's and I had just had the rather good fortune of dating one of the leading Black women in Greensboro. And as bright, intelligent and attractive as she was I thought it the highest compliment for her to actually want to invest in me. Still, none of that mattered. With all of her physical beauty she didn't have a clue. To say she was awful in bed would have been an understatement.

It's a peculiar oddity but in a man full of vim and vigor, testosterone and a liberal dose of ego that he sees no such thing as bad sex but only untapped potential when in reality there is no therapy or rehabilitation that will remedy this particular frailty.

The following day I got up and shopped for the weekend before stopping home to shower and change clothes.

"Afternoon love."

"Oooh. I like the way that sounds."

"Just calling to see if we were still on for lunch?"

"I certainly hope so. Listen. I need you to stop by Boston Market and pick up one of their rotisserie chickens on the way. How long will it take you?"

"I'm on my way."

"Oooh, I'm so excited. And I don't know if I mentioned it or not but I really enjoyed you last night. Anyway the front door's open."

I was at the house on Tower Road in twenty minutes. I couldn't understand why I was so nervous. We had already been intimate so the hard part was over. But the expectation that we were to pick up where we left off bothered me. Was that what the check had been all about? Was I now supposed to perform like a trained bear in a circus? Is this what I had committed to?

When she opened the door all my anxieties and apprehensions ceased to exist.

I opened the door to Myrtle standing on the bottom step of the spiral staircase dressed in a sheer white teddy with matching robe that did little to mask the inner workings. She had a pair of white open toed mules. I had everything to do to contain myself when she pulled my head to her hard brown nipple. I pushed the teddy to one side and took her small but ample breast into my mouth. Crushing them against the roof of my mouth she moaned.

"Are you hungry?" I asked.

"The only thing I'm hungry for is you," she said grabbing my hand and leading me up to her bedroom.

All my apprehension around performing were gone. I was ready to perform. I knew her outfit had to run a few hundred and I was mesmerized. I saw visions of Josephine Baker and Lena Horne. She was exotic in her own unique way that I have yet to define. Perhaps she was the first woman I'd met with such elegance and class. And she was extremely pleasing to the eye.

"You know I've never been in here with anyone other than my husband. Now that I think of it I've never been with another man aside from my husband."

"I feel honored." I said knowing there was no real future in her words. At least there was no future according to my plans. It had only been a couple of weeks and I got the sense that she would have a hard time telling her children about me and so I was in the shadows for the most part.

That was the day I broke the bed. I have to admit that I was frustrated. I liked her an d she liked me but there could be no future. She was content to live out her destiny and that destiny did not include me. So, on this day I wanted her to feel me. I wanted her to know what she should expect. I wanted her to know exactly what she was getting. There was some anger on my part. There was anger towards her for thinking that I would sell out for money. I was angry at myself for selling out. Had I stooped so low that I was willing to sleep with someone that I felt no love for for a few dollars?

Don't get me wrong. I liked her. In fact I was crazy about her. She was the brightest woman I have ever known. Her mind was excellent and our conversations were both inspiring and insightful. Often times I'd walk away feeling as though I had had an epiphany. That in itself would have been enough but she had so many other qualities I liked and admired and endeared her. She was the most beautiful woman I didn't want to be in the prone position with. But she had no plans for me other than being her flunky and her boy toy at her beck and call.

I liked the fact that she didn't rely solely on her looks but coupled that with the knowledge that had gotten her this far but the combination of the two had swallowed me whole. I so enjoyed the intellectual side of our relationship. It was one of the few times since I'd reached adulthood where I met a teacher extraodinaire whose life experiences ran circles around mine and who broadened my horizons daily. That was her magnet and what drew me to her and although I was conflicted being stuck with her wasn't all bad.

We traveled often. And when we traveled she picked up the tab. In fact, when we went anywhere she picked up the tab. Dinner. Hotels. Out for drinks. She picked up the tab. Despite her doing this and never demanding anything of me I felt no romantic link. I wanted to but it was more than a little obvious that I would been out there alone and if I gave way to my feelings I would just end up alone and heartbroken once again. Her only frailty was in the bedroom. If the owness falls on anyone it would have to be her husband the only other man she'd been romantically and sexually linked with. For me it only took two or three times to see that she had never been taught to kiss and

making love meant no more than disrobing, assuming the position and offering herself up.

I knew she enjoyed sex as she'd come to know it. And that was quickly apparent when we lay down together. She made no attempts to join in but lay there limp and lifeless begging me to pound it harder and harder until I had orgasm ed. I still don't know if she achieved an orgasm. I suppose this is what she was used to but I had a hard time trying to understand a man so disregarding his partner in such a manner.

One thing was for certain. Good looks didn't equate to good love. Still, I refused to be defeated. So much untapped potential was just lying there dormant, stagnant with the years passing by and no idea of the joys of lovemaking. Determined not to suffer each time we lay down together I undertook the Herculean task of rehabilitating her sexual awareness. But mostly we talked. I talked because I wanted to learn and I talked to keep her mind off sex. I knew she liked and cared about me but her role in the community had long been established. She was Mr. Wright's wife. From what she told me he was a degenerate gambler whose weakness at the time of his death were card games although he played the numbers habitually and for large sums of money. She had been with the I.R.S. for close to thirty years and was the one responsible for paying the bills and keeping everything running. Her financial portfolio continued to grow despite his gambling. Only in his mid fifties I was curious as to how he died.

"Came and went at the same time," she said with no emotion.

'It took a few minutes before her comment registered. When I didn't comment she continued.

"He died in me."

Still, I didn't respond. What could I say? My mind was racing. He probably died in his attempts to revive that dead ass pussy. He probably should have tried mouth-to-mouth. I knew that shit she was carrying was deadly. And it might have killed Mr. Wright but it wasn't going to kill me.

I kept all this inside me and grew quite cautious when the topic of sex came up. Even a simple compliment like 'you look very nice today' or 'I'm lovin' that dress' could be twisted into a sexual innuendo like 'If you like this dress you're going to love the Victoria Secret underneath. Let's go somewhere where I can show it to you.'

Most of the time I granted her wishes and she was thrilled. I enjoyed the closeness and the fact that I could call her mine with no objections from her. I also like the fact that she was loyal and would do almost anything I asked. In other words, she was there by my side through thick and thin, through epic depression and with my family in good times. In any case, not only was she thrilled when granted sex it seemed like the more she received the more her appetite grew. Realizing that she was growing sexually and being a giving person she would shower me with whatever she thought I wanted or needed. What I wanted most of all she seemed

unable to give me. I remember getting a call from her one Friday evening.

"You still out there or are you finishing up?"

"I'm heading in as we speak."

"Good day?"

"Yes, but I'm exhausted."

"Where are you now? Randleman and 85."

"Oh, good. You're not too far away. Stop by for a minute. I have something for

you."

Before I could tell her it had been a long day and all I wanted to see was my bed

she'd hung up. She was out of the way but I made my way to her house. When

she opened the door dressed for bed I sighed. I'd been duped again. How many

times had she summoned me telling me that she had something for me. When I'd

arrive I'd find her in a brand new negligee that said I am what you came for.

Tonight, however, was different. Leading me up the stairs to the den she had me sit. Returning minutes later with a veal parmigiana dinner from Vito's and a carafe of red wine. I was in heaven. I ate and drank heartily before putting my head back on the couch. She sat on the floor at my feet. I could feel her hands on my zipper. Once she had both my belt and my zipper undone she prodded me to lift up, sliding my pants down to my ankles before taking all of me into her mouth. I was shocked. Sucking it with a great deal of enthusiasm she made slurping sounds and mumbled incoherently which only heightened the mood. After a good two minutes of highly intense sucking and slurping

she jumped up, grabbed my hand and led me to her bedroom where she lay across the bed and said take me. In her employ I did as I was told.

By this time, our relationship had evolved into other areas but all were dependent on her and it would not have been in the best interest to say what was really on my mind. In the past few months I'd taken the creative license to make a bid for using the truck to start a moving company instead of letting it sit dormant from Monday til Friday. After distributing thousands of flyers we began to receive phone calls and just like that we were in business. I'd also opened the furniture booth at the flea market. She made it a point to educate me in the furniture business and I absorbed the knowledge greedily. I was making good money and was appreciative of her giving me the opportunity but her wanting sex everytime we'd meet was really beginning to wear on me. It would have been different if there was something attached to our union such as love or wanting to build a relationship. Sex if nothing else could be a conduit but never was it supposed to be an end in itself. At least that's the way I pictured it.

One evening she called to ask if I would ride with her.

"I'll have you home by nine."

It was seven-thirty then. It would be eight o'clock before she got there. I didn't mind and saw no harm spending an hour with Myrtle. And with that I got in the car. Twenty minutes later we pulled up at a motel in Burlington. This angered me to no end. It had become increasingly evident that she was so adamant about protecting her image that we'd never spent a night at a hotel in Greensboro. I was okay to lay down with and to work with but in her attempts to be discreet she would do her best not to allow our affair to be seen.

I was more than a little angry that the ride she'd asked me to take inevitably ended up at an out-of-town motel where among all my other duties and responsibilities was the responsibility of pleasing her sexually. I was use to women proclaiming their love and the give and take of partners fighting to please each other. But these pseudo kidnappings which had long since befuddled and confused me now only infuriated me.

It was late fall and the weather was bitterly cold. Myrtle was dressed for the weather with black, leather thigh high boots, a black thigh high mini skirt and a ruffled white blouse.

She was giddy with expectations and began to disrobe no sooner than she got in the room.

"Don't do that?" I said with a sternness not usually found in my voice. There was little or no emotion because the emotion that had been was now replaced with distrust and disappointment.

"Take your panties off.

When she started taking her leather bomber jacket off I again stopped her.

"Just the panties."

Always a willing student Myrtle leaned back on the bed, lifting her legs she slid her panties down to her ankles. I took them off and continued to hold her legs up. She tried handing me the lubricant but I wouldn't be needing it tonight. I forced myself into her burying my shaft deep within her. And each time I would bury myself within her she would scream and try to pull away.

"Bert! It's too much. Be gentle. You're hurting me."

I saw no difference between tonight and our normal sex but she felt the difference. I plunged deeper, harder. She grabbed the pillow and held it tightly to her mouth muffling her screams.

"Oh baby! I'm coming."

We came at the same time.

"Damn baby. What was that all about? Did I do something to you?" She said smiling sheepishly.

"That's what you wanted wasn't it? I don't get you. Most women at this juncture would either ask themselves 'how can I foster this relationship and make it better or how can I make my man happy?' but that never crossed your mind. You're more inclined to say I don't have any plans. Let me pick Bert up and get some liquor in him so he loses every inhibition and fucks me real good.

In almost everyone's life that I am somehow involved in I serve a purpose. And I willingly accept the responsibility. But I have never had someone in my life whose

sole purpose for me is just to fuck them.

And even if I did happen to come across someone who just wanted me to sleep with them it was always as a means to an end. They used it to get pregnant or to get married. But I have never had anyone willing to pay me just to have sex with them. There is no love and emotion on your part. There is no sincerity on your behalf but most of all and what hurts most is that you don't see a future for us. If this was any other area of your life you would have a goal set but where we're concerned you have no goal."

The more I spoke the harder she mashed on the gas pedal. I know she was hitting close to a hundred miles per hour now. I wasn't suicidal so I tempered the rest of what I had to say until I got out.

She cursed me out the rest of the way home dispelling my every contention. She, have her tell it, wanted more than just a physical affair but it was rather difficult with all that was on her plate. It just so happened that she was taking me to meet her mother and sister in Elizabethtown this very weekend. As far as only staying at hotels outside of Greensboro that was simply a matter of economics. Rooms were cheaper outside of the city limits.

I was quiet because I feared for my life. I was quiet because I wanted to be wrong. I wanted nothing more than for her to profess her love. Perhaps that was too much to ask for but when I saw that that wasn't possible I sought to extricate myself once

more from the eventual pain of another senseless heartbreak. We tried to find some common ground after that but with our increasing workload it was harder and harder to find time. She was drinking more and more through here and it wasn't a good look on her. When I approached her concerning her drinking she brushed me away the way a parent does when they've lost patience with a child.

"Why am I drinking?" she said hitting the bottle of Hennessey that had become a mainstay of the bar underneath her seat.

"White people have a problem they go to a shrink. Black people have problems they go to the liquor store. Me? I've been to both and well frankly I prefer the liquor store."

There was no working with her now. Jobs were plentiful but she had all but abandoned the business. I was forced to give the bid on a potential job, hire and pay the workers and do the actual move. I was trying to work my regular job, run her flea market booth as well as my own and take care of the moving business.

I did go to Elizabethtown but after the heated argument on the way back from that motel in Burlington things were hardly the same anymore. We still slept together occasionally but we weren't nearly as friendly as we had been.

One day after making good love she turned to me.

"How did you get to be so good in bed?"

"I don't know that I'm any different than any other man out there. I think the only difference is that I always put my partners happiness first and foremost. I cannot be pleased until she is both pleased and satisfied. If I'm in bed chances are that I love her and so her happiness will always be paramount coming even before my own happiness. I guess that would be the key."

I don 't know how the night ended but somehow I think my words went in vain.

Mary Hargrove

My parents owned the only Black restaurant in downtown Fayetteville. To many it was a haven for good food and spirited conversation.

I was teaching middle school at the time along with working at a group home and writing a weekly sports column for the Challenger newspaper. In my spare time, if there was any, I usually busied myself by helping my parents about the restaurant.

During the early evenings many of the workers and professors from Fayetteville State College would stop by for dinner on their way home. My buddy, Samad and i would stand outside the restaurant and watch the women as they left work and waited in line for the bus home. We were fairly young then and both of us were intent on finding our soul mate.

"Damn! Little shorty is fine as hell. Check her out. Pretty legs, gorgeous lips. She's gotta have a man."

"Only one way to find out. And if you don't I will."

Not to be out done I stepped into a realm I was not comfortable with. I've always been shy so for me to step up to the plate was a major coup on Samad's part.

"Hey. My name is Bert," I said sticking out my hand.

She smiled and took my hand.

"Mary," she said smiling.

"Nice to meet you Mary. Do you work downtown?"

"Yes. But it's only a temp job I got through an agency so it probably won't last but another couple of weeks. And what do you do?"

"I'm a middle school teacher."

She looked puzzled.

"Oh, you're trying to figure out the apron. It's a little part time gig. I come down after school to help the Brown's with the clean up."

"So, Black people own it?"

"You know it wasn't long ago Black folks weren't even allowed on Hay Street. You know that's where they used to auction off slaves," she said pointing to the Market House which sat in the middle of the town square less than a block away."

"Yes ma'am."

"That's beautiful though. It's really nice to see Black people finally getting apiece of the pie. And now that I know I've gotta stop in and check it out."

"Why don't you come in. I'll fix you a meal to die for. C'mon you know you don't want to go home and have to cook."

"I still have to go home and fix dinner for my son."

"You have a son? How old is he?"

"He just turned fifteen."

"Is he a good kid?"

"The best and I'm not just saying that because I'm his mother. He really is a good kid. But seriously I'll be in Friday. It's payday."

"You don't have to worry about that. Dinner's on me."

"Are you sure?"

"Not a problem. I'm in pretty good with the owners. They love me," I said smiling broadly.

"I have to pick up my son tonight. Can I get a raincheck?"

"No problem. I'll see you tomorrow then?"

"God permitting," she said smiling as her bus pulled up.

"Nice meeting you Mary."

"Same here."

The next day at right around the same time I looked but she was nowhere to be found. The restaurant was busy with the regulars pouring in to grab a little something to get them through the night. And then there were those that would come in and order a bowl of pintos and a slice of cornbread just. My parents brought something new to Fayetteville which was traditionally a southern bastion of hatred and ignorance. Glorified for being independent free thinking politically progressive Blacks who had weathered the storm of racism and discrimination. They were on the front lines during the Civil Rights Movement and continued where the movement ceased to exist.

In any case, I washed the dishes, cleaned the grill and put the food away. And still there was no Mary. I wasn't sure what the night held for me but if there was one thing I did not want to do it was going home alone. My life had become monotonous. All I did was work.

"What's up Black man?"

I knew the familiar greeting all too well.

"What up Samad?"

"Coolin'. Just coolin'. But listen remember the little chocolate shorty with the nice hips you pushed up on yesterday?"

"Yeah, what up with her? She was supposed to stop in tonight."

"She's outside double parked in the red truck."

"Good look Samad," I said as I dashed out the door.

"Hey Mary,"

"Listen Bert. I'm gonna need to get another raincheck. My dad hasn't been feeling well as of late so I need to drop by and check on him. You wanna ride with me?"

"Let me run in and tell them that I'm leaving. Why don't you pull around the corner. I'll be right out."

Minutes later I jumped into the old beat up Toyota pick up.

"Have to pick up my son from school and drop him at home. It'll only take a minute."

"Do what you have to do Mary. Don't worry about me. I just came along for the ride."

Mary pulled up in front of a young Black boy. Seeing his mother the boy started grinning. His face dropped when he saw me. I got out so he could get in.

"Hey man. How's my favorite son?"

"I'm good."

"How was school today?"

"It was alright."

"Oh, I'm sorry. This is Mr. Bert. Bert this is my son Jordan."

"Nice to meet you Jordan. I've heard a lot of good things about you. Any relation between you and my man?"

"You mean Michael? No. I'm not related but I do play ball," he said smiling.

"You play for Westover?"

"No. I missed try outs. My mom and I moved here after the season started."

"You a big basketball fan?"

"The biggest but Michael Jordan's not my favorite player. I mean I like him. I like him a lot. I've got all his cards except his rookie card and second year card."

"Oh you're a collector?"

"Is he? Jordan's taken over the guest room with all of his cards."

"Is that right?"

"Yes sir. But most of my cards are only two or three years old so they're not worth a whole lot."

"Not now but they will be. Be patient Jordan. All things in time. Who's your favorite player?"

"I think it's a tie between Jason Williams of the Kings and Allen Iverson."

"I hear you."

You could learn a lot from observing a child. And though I didn't know Mary all that well I knew one thing. She had instilled some traditional values in her son. He was both mannerable and respectful in an age where kids weren't and adults would excuse them saying that the kids today are different. No. What was different were the parents who spent less time and really weren't involved in their children's lives. Jordan was strong and secure and from their interaction I knew she instilled love as well.

Mary pulled up in front of the tiny green and white house in Loch Lemond.

"Change your clothes, do your homework and your chores. If you get hungry there are some TV dinners in the freezer."

"Okay ma."

"It was nice meeting you Jordan. And maybe if you're not doing anything this weekend we can go card shopping."

"Oh ma, can we?"

"I don't know. We'll see how the rest of the week goes. How did you do on your biology test?"

"I got a ninety two."

"That's what I'm talking about," she said grabbing him and hugging him.

"So, can we go?"

"I'll let you know. Now let me go so I can get back."

"Okay. See you Mr. Bert."

"Seems like you made a new friend."

"I sure hope so. I don't like making enemies. I like him. He's both mannerable and respectful."

"He better be. He doesn't have much choice."

"Where's his father?"

"I would like to say he's up at Princeton working on a government project dealing with thermo-nuclear but I'd be lying."

"So, should I ask?"

"It's no secret. He's been incarcerated for the last six years."

"Wow," was the best I could muster.

All was quiet now as we rode for the better part of an hour through a North Carolina I would never have envisioned. Small, one room, wooden shacks lined the narrow two lane highway. The shacks looked uninhabitable but I noticed clouds of smoke coming from several chimneys. At the end of the row of shacks were acre after acre of cotton and tobacco fields. From this vantage point it wasn't hard to imagine African slaves standing side-by-side picking cotton in the midday sun for some wealthy southern landholder.

My thoughts were suddenly interrupted when Mary turned onto a dirt road. Driving no more than a few hundred feet into the woods we pulled up in front of one those shacks we'd just passed. Walking in the front door Mary greeted her father, a relatively young man about fifty with a huge smile and hug before introducing me. I stood there speechless. I'd seen documentaries on slavery. I couldn't understand why people were still living like this in the wealthiest nation in the world. It seemed somehow surreal as if this were some sort of reenactment of earlier times.

In the middle of the room sat a cast iron pot-bellied stove. There was a hole in the roof and I assumed this was to let the smoke out. The windows had no glass or screens but were instead wooden windows which swung open to let the sun in when it was nice and were pulled shut to keep the rain, and snow out. The floor was made of raw wood, coarse and rough. There was one handmade wooden chair and I saw no bathroom facilities suggesting that somewhere in the not too far distance was an outhouse. I was still in a state of shock when we left the old man. I couldn't understand people living under these conditions in this day and age.

"Did you grow up there?"

"No. But it was similar. When my mother died my father took that place. Said he didn't need a three bedroom when it was just him so he moved there. He sharecrops, picking cotton and cropping tobacco when the time comes. But yeah, my sisters and I grew up in a place like that, just bigger. We didn't have much but we were happy."

I listened to her and thought back to a trip I had taken to the island of Jamaica. I was up in the mountains talking, smoking and philosphying with my new found Rastafarian friends when one of them commented that I probably wasn't used to living like this. He went on to to say that although Americans had the two car garage and the flat screen TV they were poor in spirit but Jamaicans who had little were rich in spirit so I understood when Mary said they were happy. Mary had seen both worlds and still held a special allegiance to her foundation and was proud of her origins. I appreciated this and was even more fond of her after this venture.

We met the next day for a late lunch. We talked and laughed. Laughter came easily for Mary. She must have enjoyed lunch as well since she turned to me and said.

"What are you doing later?"

"I didn't have anything planned."

"Well, as the young folks say, 'Let's link up.'"

"Oooh that sounds good. I think I have rent money for one night."

"Stop being so fresh," Mary said pretending to take a swing at me.

"My bad. Seriously though, why don't you just meet me at the house.

"Okay. I'm gonna run home and check on Jordan."

"Okay. Here's the key to the house. I've got to run down and clean up the restaurant. You'll be there long before I will."

"Tell you what. Why don't I wash while you do the grills and the floor.

"You sure?"

"I'm sure. This way I get to spend more time with you."

I couldn't believe she was volunteering to help me. I welcomed her company as much as her help.

An hour later I turned to her.

" Do you want to sit while I finish up? I need you to save your energy. I have other things planned for you."

"Can't wait,"she said smiling.

"Boy that was quick." My mother commented as she came into the kitchen.
 "We've got to get Mary in here more often. We might get home at a decent hour."

We finished up and Mary followed me to the house. I was exhausted. Noticing Mary handed me the remote before leaning over and kissing me. In the weeks that followed I came to the realization that a kiss was all it took to get her in the mood. She was a fireball and a kiss could easily lead to her ripping off my shirt. To say she was a fireball is an understatement. What she was was spontaneous.

Afterwards we went back to my house. Pulling up in the church parking lot next door to my apartment Mary turned to me. I was a little puzzled as to why she hadn't pulled into the driveway but it wasn't long before I had my answer. It was early evening, dark enough for us to go unnoticed. Turning to me Mary kissed me deeply, passionately while adeptly unbuckling my belt. I was hard just from the mounting tension she exuded when she threw her leg over me, straddling me. Warm and moist she took me in her easily.

"Wouldn't you rather take this inside?"

"If I wanted to be inside I would be inside. Now hush and enjoy the ride," she said taking all of me and slamming down hard on me with each stroke. Throwing her head back, eyes closed I knew she was lost in the moment. I watched as the beads of perspiration gathered about her nipples which were fully exposed now and pressed against my face. The bridge of her nose now held beads of perspiration as well and I knew she was on the verge of climaxing.

"Damn baby. I forgot just how good it could be. Oh baby I think I'm about to bust. Oh baby, I don't want to come. It feels so good I don't want it to ever stop. Baby, promise me we can do this again before the night's over."

She was holding on now. Holding on for dear life refusing to come until I promised that I would take her there again.

"I promise."

Moments later she screamed and I knew she had come good and hard. I felt a warm wet wetness between my legs.

"Oh baby, I'm so sorry. You really took me there. You made me pee on myself."

"Good thing we're close to home."I said trying to put her at ease but she was undeterred by the wetness.

"We can go home in a minute but let's not be hasty. Besides the damage is already done," she said straddling me again. and sliding down on my rigid shaft once more. I saw headlights in the mirror and wondered if I should mention it. She had a way of making her vagina contract squeezing me with every stroke. It was incredible.

"There's a car approaching Mary."

"I see it," she said pumping harder now. "That's it baby. Fuck this pussy baby." It was the first time I'd heard Mary curse and I have to admit it turned me on.

A few minutes she was screaming again.

"Baby I'm coming again. Tell me you want me. Tell me it's good to you. Baby..."

When it was over she moved back into the driver's seat.

"I'm pretty sure those were the police. I have a feeling they'll be circling around. Let me drop you off and run and check on Jordan. It shouldn't take me more than twenty minutes at the most. Well, that is if you still want to see me."

"I always want to see you, Mary."

"Tell me the truth. You're such a nice guy that even if you didn't want to see me or were dead tired you wouldn't tell me."

"Trust me," I lied. "I would let you know. I'm not that nice."

"So you want me to come back?"

"I never want you to leave." Smiling broadly she tried to kiss me but I jumped out of the truck before she had a chance to.

"No, no, no. I've already had one close call tonight and you know what your kisses lead to."

"I'm not sure but I will find out when I get back. And I suggest you take full advantage tonight since I'll be out of commission next week."

"And what does that mean?"

"My sister Theresa is coming from New York to spend a week. I don't think I will be able to see you while she's here."

"When's she coming?"

"She arrives tomorrow at four on Amtrak and I was hoping you could pick her up and take her to the restaurant until I get off."

"So you're spending the night tonight?"

"I hadn't planned on it," she said smiling.

"Plan on it."

"Alright well let me check on Jordan and grab something for work tomorrow."

An hour later we lay in the bed draped around each other, sex funky and spent.

"I think I'm falling in love with you Mary."

"Are you falling in love with me or is it what I bring to the table?"

I thought about what she said and wondered if there wasn't some truth to it. Was our relationship just one of convenience and good sex? Perhaps she was right. One thing was for sure I should have never made this comment following a roll in the hay.

We spent the night together and made good love several more times before the night was over. We slept in each other's arms and for the first time in a very long time I felt complete.

Funny but after months of being in each other's company I still found her to be quite refreshing. I even considered marriage. Now she may question my words or the timing but the days had flown by and still it felt new. Being around her with her upbeat attitude was wonderful but I told myself no lies and I was falling in love if I hadn't already fallen. That morning as we got dressed for work she came to me.

"I don't know if you know but I'm really struggling with Jordan, the house and just trying to make ends meet. I was talking to my seargent in the reserves the other day

and he was telling me that I could go active for two years, learn a trade, get a paycheck and a housing allowance. It's a good deal and better than anything I'm seeing out here. The only problem is Jordan. I don't want to keep upending him every time he gets settled. It's happened far too many times already. So, I was wondering if you'd consider keeping him. You know he adores you and I know he could use a strong Black man as a role model right through here."

I sat there dumbfounded. I was honored. The same woman who questioned my love the night before was now asking me to care for her most prized possession. I wanted her love and I guess this was her admission. At least that's what I chose to believe. She wanted me to be the legal guardian of her only child. Still, I couldn't just answer. This required some serious thought. I hadn't known her long enough to warrant her entrusting me with her child. And with two children of my own I wasn't sure I wanted the added responsibility of raising a teenager.

"Wow. That's deep. In a matter of minutes I've lost a woman and gained a child," I said doing my best to change the topic.

"You haven't lost anything. I'm just going away to work to make life better for everyone involved. I'll be sending checks regularly. And you serve to save money too. If you move into the house then there's no need for you to be paying rent. You can put what you're paying for rent now in the bank. Well, at least think about it. I need to tell my sergeant something one way or another by Monday."

"I'll let you know something by the weekend. But I see nothing that would make me say no."

"Oh baby. You're a godsend," she said grinning and kissing me long and hard on the mouth before grabbing my belt and snatching my pants down to my knees.

"Take them off," she said bending over and stepping out of her panties.

"Baby I'm going to be late."

"Then you'd better hurry." When my pants were completely off she looked at me.

"Now sit down."

I did as I was told and she quickly approached me lifting her skirt and easing down on my erect member.

"Damn baby. I don't know if I'm crazy about you for you being you or if I'm just in love with the way you make love to me."

"I certainly hope it's the first one and not just because you like sex and we're good in bed."

"Oh baby. I can't lie. You do have me craving your ass. Ooooh baby. That's my spot. Come on baby. Fuck me."

I wanted to tell her I loved her but thought about the timing. I'd already made that mistake. But with that thought I realized that she was going through the same thing. The sex was damn good often clouding boundaries. Now here we were both asking the same question. Were we crazy about each other or had our hellacious love making sessions glossed over everything. I was hardly in denial and even though the sex was splendid there was no doubt that I loved Mary for a myriad of reasons all of them as important as our lovemaking. By the time I got to work I was exhausted. I wondered how Mary was holding up. By the time I got off all I wanted to do was head down to the

restaurant and go upstairs and take a nap. I was well on my way to do just that when I got a text from Mary reminding me to pick up her sister Theresa from the train station. I wasn't all that fond of meeting new people and as tired as I was I was in no mood to meet Mary's sister or anyone else for that matter.

Theresa got off the train somewhat apprehensively looking first left and then right for someone she hadn't yet met. She had no idea who I was but I had a pretty good description of her. I didn't know her. What I did know was that she was tall, close to six feet and black as the night. I remember Mary describing her.

"You want to know what my sister looks like? Okay close your eyes and picture a beautifully, majestic, African queen. That's Theresa. No other description is required. She's exotic and regal. You're going to love her. Just don't let her overwhelm you. Remember Mary's the one who butters your toast."

"I know you didn't just go there. You insulted both me and your sister."

"Calm down Mr. Brown. I'm just teasing. Besides my sister and I have had a pact since we first started dating's that says we don't talk to or flirt with each others man."

And still with all that a given I was still nervous about picking up a perfect stranger. I was supposed to make her feel warm and comfortable when I was as uncomfortable as I could possibly be.

I stood inside the vestibule of the Amtrak waiting for the passengers to disembark. I watched as passenger after passenger got off but not a one resembled the image I had drawn in my mind when I felt a slight tap on my shoulder.

"You must be Bert?"

To be perfectly honest the description Mary had given me of an African queen fell far below the woman standing before me. The woman before me was nothing short of a goddess. And it s my belief that most African queens would have abdicated their thrones for Theresa's looks. Jet black with keen Ethiopian features that somehow made her exotic looking and would not allow me to speak at first.

"Mary told me you were beautiful but that was an understatement. I hope you don't mind me asking but how old are you?"

"I'm twenty-nine. Why do you ask?"

"I was thinking. You'd be just perfect for my son."

"And how old is your son?"

"Two going on three but he's very mature for his age."

Theresa responded with a warm, hearty laugh.

"You hungry?"

"I'm starved. They served food on the train but I refuse to spend three dollars for a plain bagel and some cream cheese."

"I hear you. I'm going to take you to the best little soul food restaurant this side of Sylvia's. I work there part-time so you come in and have a seat and let me fix you a good meal. All I want you to do is sit back and relax. Don't worry about a thing. I work there and am in fairly good with the owners."

"Goodness. I never expected such service."

"Only the very best for you my queen." I said going into the kitchen to fix her meal. When I'd finished she stared at a plate complete with baby back ribs, macaroni and cheese, collard greens and cornbread. I also brought her a Mason jar full of freshly squeezed lemonade.

When she was finished with her meal I topped it off with homemade peach cobbler and a scoop of vanilla ice cream.

"You know I grew up here and heard about southern hospitality but this is the first time I've experienced it."

"Perhaps you've been traveling in the wrong circles."

"Perhaps you're right."

"Listen I have a friend. He works down the block at Wachovia. He's a bank manager. Want me to call him and see what he's doing tonight?"

"I guess Mary didn't tell you. That's one of the reasons I'm here."

"No. She didn't mention it to me."

"I just got out of an abusive relationship with my kid's father after five years. I don't think I'm capable of having a relationship with a man right through here."

"You and I seem to be hitting it off okay."

"It's always okay until feelings are shared. That's when it starts to get complicated."

"We don't seem to have any problem."

"You're right but as soon as a man sees that I'm in love and vulnerable they take my kindness as weakness. I've been with my kids father for close to six years and we were building. He was talking of moving and marriage. And then about two weeks ago I went to my bank and found out my account was overdrawn, his was overdrawn and the same with our joint account. I can't believe he left not just me but our three kids without a cent and destitute. Who does that? What kind of man does that?"

"I don't know Theresa. But you can't throw the baby out with the bath water. That's one man. There are a lot of great guys out there."

"Name one other than yourself."

"Come on Theresa. There are lots of other good men out there. You just happened to pick a loser."

Before she could finish her thought Mary walked in. The sisters hugged and laughed so glad were they to see each other.

"I was just telling Bert to give me his number in case you had brain cramps, reservations or a change of heart. Seriously though, Mary you've got a winner here. It's hard to find a nice guy and a gentleman. I think you've found both."

"Believe me. You don't have to tell me sister. I get down on my knees everyday and thank the good Lord for putting him in my life. And Jordan loves him too.

I think he and Jordan spend more time together than he spends with me. Come on. I know you must be beat. I'll tell you all the good juicy stuff on the way to the house," Mary said winking at me.

"And the food... I need to tell your boss about the food and the top notch service. You never know it may lead to a raise. They seem really cool and they seem to adore you."

"What are you talking about Tee Tee?"

"Bert's boss, the owners, see the couple behind the counter."

"Girl. Don't tell me he got you too," Mary said laughing. "That's Mr. and Mrs. Brown. Those are Bert's parents."

"Oh, no you didn't," Theresa said smiling and shaking her fist at me. I walked the two around the corner to the little red truck and bid them a good night.

Two days past before I heard from Mary.

"Hey Bert. How are you? I'm sorry I haven't had a chance to call. Between my father and Theresa it's been hectic but listen. I'm in a jam and need your help. They asked me to work tonight and I know Theresa doesn't want to be sitting in the house alone. If you're not doing anything I was wondering if you could go by and pick her up; maybe go out and do something. I have about forty or fifty

dollars. That should do

dinner if you two want to go out and grab something to eat. Just stop by and pick

it up when you get finished."

"Never a problem sweetie. Call and tell her I'm on my way."

"You're the best bay."

"Oh, you're going to pay."

"If you say so."

"Love you Mary."

"K."

Never, Not once had I ever heard her repeat the words, 'I love you' and still I did

her bartering hoping that one day it would flow just as easily as 'Bert. I'm in a

jam.'

Picking up Theresa turned out to be a blessing in disguise. She was bubbly and exuberant on what would have otherwise been a boring night.

"I hope Mary didn't disturb your night. I told her I was cool but she's always on this guilt trip. Nothing is ever good enough. She feels she can make it better. I was cool sitting at home and watching The Voice. Guess her maternal instincts just took over."

"Truth is I was exhausted and was going to head home, take a shower and lie across the bed and watch the idiot box until it watched me."

"So, you did have plans?"

"If you wanna call those plans."

"They are or should say they were. I am sorry. Mary's my sister and I love her but she's not the most considerate person in the world. She's also not too bright. No woman with any kind of common sense puts her man in the hands of another woman."

"But you're not just another woman. You're her sister."

"A sister is not immune to the human frailties of lust and temptation. All you'd have to do is tempt me."

I couldn't believe my ears and it must have shown on my face.

"Oh, come on Bert. I'm just playing. This is my sister we're talking about."

She tried to sound convincing but the cat was out of the bag now and I knew that if I in any way made an overture she would have gladly taken me up on it. All she needed was a little encouragement.

I in no way think it is me specifically but the idea of a man that would cater to her, love her and enjoy her making her the central theme in his life. That's what I symbolized and not even her sister would deter her this time. How long had she been in waiting. Six years this time. But never would that happen again. No. This time she would wrap him up so tightly in her love that he would not be able to leave.

"Can we just go to your house and chill instead of going out?"

"Not a problem. Those were my plans before Mary called me."

Once at home I showed Theresa the lay of the land and gave her the remote. And after making herself a drink she made herself over to the loveseat and sat beside me.

"Bert I want you to turn and look at me."

Doing as I was instructed I looked into her hazel eyes and became completely unhinged.

"Yes ma'am."

"I want to ask you a question and I want you to be perfectly honest with me."

"Okay. I think I can do that."

"Okay. Tell me this. Do you find me attractive?"

"Why would you ask me that when you already know the answer."

"I'm asking you. I'm not interested what the rest of the world thinks."

"And you know I do. Now I have a question for you Theresa."

"I'm listening."

"Why would you ask me something like that when you know I'm in a relationship with your sister?"

"Because the only way I know if I appeal to a man is to ask him."

"And why is my opinion so important to you?"

"Let's just say I have my reasons. I wish I could share them with you but I'd be out-of-line if I did but trust me you and I are destined to be close friends."

"So, you're not going back to New York?"

"Not if I can find a job in the next few weeks. I'm tired of fighting the crowds. I guess Im tired of whole rat race. It was fun when I was in my early twenties and didn't

have kids but now it's just hectic. So, I figure I need to start making friends and start networking. And from what my sister tells me you write and work for the Black newspaper here. And I am now your new typist. Don't worry I come free. That is there is no charge for my typing. What I do want is for you to put my name out there. I'm an excellent secretary."

"That's fine. I am still curious as to what you're not telling me."

"I try not to get involved in my sister's business just like I wouldn't want her involved in mine but be patient Bert. All things in time."

This conversation with Theresa hung over my head like a bad dream for the rest of the week until Mary called putting my mind at ease and invited me to a cook out on Saturday. It had been close a week since I'd seen Mary so I was ecstatic.

For the cook out I bought ten or twelve T-bone steaks. Then I threw on a pair of jeans, a crisp white Oxford and a pair of penny loafers and headed to the cook-out. I arrived to a nice crowd of twenty-five or thirty people none of which I knew.

"Hey Bert."

I was glad to see a familiar face.

"Hey Theresa. What's up?"

Her all too familiar smile was gone and I could see something was troubling her deeply.

"I've been sitting here waiting for you. Where's your car?"

"Bout halfway down the block. Why what's up?"

"We need to talk. Come on. Let's walk."

Minutes later we arrived at the car. She hadn't said a word on the way to the car.

"Are you gonna tell me what's going on?"

"Open the door Bert."

When we were seated Theresa took both my hands in hers. I watched as her eyes welled with tears.

"What's wrong sweetheart?" I said in hopes of consoling her. I sensed the type of grief she was feeling and wanted to throw my arms around her but it would have been just my luck that Mary would have walked up wondering why I was all hugged up with her sister. The best I could do was to find out what was really bothering her and perhaps give Mary a call and see if we couldn't find some solution. But first I had to know.

"Talk to me Theresa. Tell me what's really going on. I can't have my long lost sister returning home to tears and heartbreak," I said smiling before I took both her hands and held them in a vain attempt to comfort her.

"Bert. Mary's husband got out and came home yesterday. I told her to call and tell you. She knows his ass is crazy. And he knows all about you because that's all Jordan's been talking about since he got home.

"Why didn't she just tell me?"

"I don't know Bert. I told her to."

"You think I should go in and talk to her?"

"No. I only say that because that fool she married doesn't have the sense of a two year old. And she doesn't either. I told her that she would have to be out of her mind to let you get away. And Lord knows not for this ignorant, ass jailbird. My mother would roll over in her grave if she could see this crazy shit. Mary's always doing dumb shit. She had a four year scholarship to Fayetteville State to run track and what does she do. She hangs out with this piece of trash who has never had her best interest at heart and gets pregnant. Threw a four year scholarship away, a hundred thousand dollars out the window."

"Listen Theresa. I thank you for the heads up and saving me the embarrassment. It's been a long day. I think I'm gonna head home."

"I am truly sorry for having to be the bearer of bad news but what's important is your perspective. How do you see the glass? Is it half empty or half full? You may have lost a girlfriend but you've gained a friend. Which is more invaluable

"Have to think about that. I have a lot to think about today."

"By the way, what do you drink?"

"Chivas Regal."

"Okay. I'll call you later to check on you. You gonna be alright?"

"God willing. I should be."

When I got home I broke down and cried. It made no sense to me. All she had to do was call and talk to me. I was crushed. By now she had to know I stopped by and still there was no call from her. I wondered how anyone could be so cold after having spent almost everyday together for months.

I don't know how long I sat in the vestibule of my apartment revisiting the past months over and over just trying to make sense of it all. I would've probably been there half the night if Theresa hadn't called.

". I'm at the liquor store. What do you feel like?"

" you decide is fine with me. The door's open. I'm going to take a

d the door close.

"Yeah, sweetie it's me. Ice or no ice?"

"No ice. I'll be right down. I'm just getting out of the shower."

"Don't rush. I'll bring it to you."

I grabbed my robe, threw it on and headed to my room where Theresa sat on the edge of my bed looking positively elegant in her black, suede trench and six inch black heels.

"You look very nice tonight."

"Thank you. I was kinda hoping you would notice."

"Where are you going tonight?"

"I was hoping this would be my first and last stop. I thought that maybe if I got dressed up I could distract you and take your mind off the madness. I really hope you're not sweating Mary's crazy ass," she said handing me a glass of Chivas which I quickly downed.

"It's crossed my mind once or twice," I lied. "But for the life of me I don't understand."

"And chances are you never will but let's not think any more of that. Let me see if I can take you to a place a little bit more pleasant," she said standing and letting the trench coat fall to the floor revealing a body as black as the night.

CPSIA information can be obtained
at www.ICGtesting.com
Printed in the USA
LVOW09s1743140917
548744LV00007B/376/P